I0640026

Heroes for the People: Realization

Eric McEllen

Copyright © 2018 Eric McEllen
All rights reserved.
ISBN:
978-1732388611

Chapter One: Loner

The hood of his jacket hid most of his face. Just the rims of his sunglasses and stubble of his unshaven face protruded into sight. He walked slowly and deliberately, glancing out of the corner of his eye into the windows of the stores lining the street. Breaking news was being blasted on all the television screens encased in the windows. Something was happening in the middle of the city, some man in a costume. This didn't concern him, so he decided to carry on and just keep an ear out for now. He reached into his jacket pockets, fumbling around looking for any hint of cigarettes that might still exist in his possession. Nothing, but the crumbled tobacco dust in the pointed of the pockets. The same results for his dingy and worn blue jeans. Just an empty lighter. He rummaged through his caramel, cracked and weathered satchel. Just countless scribbles on scraps of papers pushed into notebooks and folders. A sneer developed on his face. He would have to interact with ordinary people without the dulling sensation from nicotine gripped between his teeth. His eyes set upwards, scanning the block for a convenience store. He continued to deliberately maneuver among the crowd, blending in, unknown.

"There's a man that has emerged from the helicopter," shouted a random reporter from each TV, "he's dressed…. In what looks like a green wetsuit? Is that? It seems he has dollar signs on his chest….it looks like he's coming towards us….he wants to talk to us!"

Still nothing. Nothing to worry himself about. No need to expose himself, especially to the media. He continued to move past the wall of TVs and ducked into the nearest convenience store. Like normal members of society, he started to wander up and down the aisles. Picking up random items and setting them back down. He had already eaten today, no need to be greedy. But tobacco. He was cranky and irritable. Yes, he needed nicotine to soothe his crowded mind. He set down powdered doughnuts, something had caught his eye. Abnormality. A man, mid-thirties, with vomit soaked and stained dumpster salvaged clothes. This man was focused, vacant. Dangerous. Human behavior is funny. As amusing as this could be, the homeless man, catty corner to the register, was about to do something stupid.

Blaring from the TV's, "Dear people of this good city!" the suited green man cheered. "I am here to protect and defend you!"

The register clerk turned around to find the homeless man's arm outstretched, trying to keep a revolver steady. "P-p-p-put the money," the homeless man wiped his face with the sleeve of his other arm, "money! Out of the register!"

Slowly the man in the hood crept forward. Desperate people were unpredictable. But he needed to get closer. The cash register flung open as the attendant started to clamber through it as if he couldn't completely close his hands. The hooded man was close enough. He quickly reached up and placed his right hand on the revolver.

It happened in a split second. The same act of flexing a bicep or the ab muscles. A quick push and his eyes dilated. His vision blurred almost completely. He felt weightless. His right hand clenched into a fist, and the revolver crumpled, like when someone stands onto an aluminum can. He relaxed, and his vision returned. He was mere inches away from the homeless man. Both the homeless man and cashier seemed to be in shock. In an instant reaction, the homeless man reared back his hand and screamed, "Yearrrgh!"

The hooded man instinctively flexed again, and after a sharp short jab in the direction of the homeless man, he heard a crunch and a loud crash. As he relaxed and his vision returned, he saw the homeless man unconscious and embedded through the glass door of the milk fridge. He turned to the cashier. The cashier's eyes were wide. His mouth open. His jaw was quivering.

The hooded man looked up, and in a calm and soothing voice announced, "I need cigarettes."

The cashier turned and with one arm pushed a half dozen packs onto the counter. The hooded man made it known, "I don't have any money."

The cashier, with both hands, pushed the packs forward. Some of which fell onto the floor. The hooded man picked them up, put them into his satchel, and turned to leave. He stopped and looked back at the cashier and in a low voice said, "And a lighter."

The cashier grabbed a handful of lighters that were next to him and chucked them at the hooded man. They hit him and fell to the floor. He bent down slowly and picked them up, put one into his satchel and kept the other in his hand, then left the store. He didn't blame the cashier. This was a normal response to seeing someone crush a revolver with their bare hand. Then punch someone across the room through a glass fridge door. The hooded man stood outside the store, near the TV's, pulled out a cigarette, lit it and took a nice long relaxing throat burning drag off it. That's better.

TV blared, "So what brings you to the middle of the city Mr...... what should 'this city' call you?"

"My name is Franchise! The protector of this city! I am in search of like-minded individuals with similar gifts."

This man was heavier set. He was Hispanic, with a Mexican accent, roughly 5'9 and 200 lbs. His posture was arrogant. He spoke with his hands and most of his body, which was covered from his neck down in skin tight material, mostly green. He had yellowish accents to include a giant dollar sign on his chest. His face was exposed except for goggles covering his eyes. At first glance, he had dollar signs on the outside of each lens, but you could see through to his eyes. There was more to his outfit. On his left arm, he had a giant metal dollar sign and what looked like several yellow hockey pucks on his belt. Some sort of back pack incorporated into the back of his costume. Two hoses run from the bottom of his backpack, they hug the back of his legs and feed into his boots, which appeared to be platforms of some kind. Franchise continued to bask in the attention of the reporters.

In the back, near the helicopter that Franchise got off, a little girl was standing next to it with an older man. The older man was taller and gaunt. He wore a leather vest and old red baron style leather cap and goggles. He sported a full-face mustache and beard that hid his mouth. He was leaning up against the chopper with his arms crossed and appeared to be annoyed. The girl standing next to him was also in a costume. She was a young black girl, maybe 14 to 16. She was 5'5 roughly 100 lbs. She wore a purple long sleeve material with a black "F" on the chest. From her belt to her boots, her costume was also glossy black, and had a cowl that lead into a cape. Her hood was down, and her hair was pulled back into a tight bun. She was wide eyed and her head swiveled constantly looking around at her surroundings. She looked out of place.

With a plastic smile, Franchise gazed into the camera and stated, "And we're looking for any, and all, heroes to join us and stand up against the people who aim to harm this fair city. We've come to this location today in search of the one they call Loner."

Loner's ears perked up, and he cocked an eyebrow. He had been careful and kept a low profile. There was no chance. He looked up to see the giant gathering near the center of the city. Plain sight. That was where he needed to be. He started maneuvering with the growing crowd. Just another bystander. Trying to catch a glimpse at the freak show. Clambering and inching forward, his pace remained the same, so as not to bring attention to himself. Steadily pulling on the end of his cigarette, he flicked it in front of him and stepped out the fading ember. He had reached the outside of the growing circle. The open-eyed pedestrians trying to absorb an image of abnormality, as if to take a mental souvenir with them. Loner needed to know that this man was harmless. Possibly a prankster. Hopefully just an attention seeker. Please let it be nothing. No cameras. No witnesses. Please be a harmless lunatic.

Franchise continued to ramble, a cheery rambling that reminded Loner of a game show host or a used car salesman. Franchise was cut off by one of the numerous reporters, "Franchise.... Franchise.... do you have a power?"

A smirk grew on Franchise's face as if to say of course I do. "Yes, dear citizen, I have a gift." The crowd exploded with cheers and chanting, they become crazed and craved an answer. "What is it Franchise?" croaked a reporter. Franchise looked at his feet, with a full blown smile.

He looked up through the top of his goggles, "You really wanna know?" he asked eagerly. The crowd chanted "YES" in unison. "I said do you really wanna know!?!" he shouted back as he brought his hand up to cup his ear in the fashion that a professional wrestler would rile up a crowd. And for some reason, it worked.

The crowd squealed with joy and excitement. And without warning, he placed his left hand on his hip and struck his right fist into the air. He gave a slight bend in his knees, and a flash emerged from his boots. As a small white cloud drifted away, Franchise was seen eight feet in the air, with two little glowing patches on either sole of his boots. They looked like the gentle glow of the top of a birthday candle as they emitted a WHHIIIRRRR sound. He now had both hands on his hips and was in a full belly laugh.

"Dear people of this city," he began, "I have the gift of intellect."

The crowd stirred. The awe from seeing a hefty man rise into the air by the very boots he wore wavered as the simple people tried to comprehend intellect as a superpower. The confusion was verbalized in various forms throughout the crowd which caused the smile to leave Franchise's face. He descended slowly and walked towards a nearby reporter.

"No, no, no, you see, I am able to comprehend complex information....look I've even created my own equipment," he begged in desperation.

This man was an idiot Loner thought to himself. Harmless, playing dress up, trying to get attention. Harmless. Loner turned and started to break away from the crowd. He was no threat. Need to keep making up ground. Need to find more information.

"So why are you looking for this Loner character?" chirped a reporter.

"Oh yes," Franchise started, "the Loner is quite possibly the strongest man in our world. I wish to demonstrate the awesome power of our gifts, in front of....YOU!" he shouted as he lifted himself up again with his boots with his arms outstretched.

The crowd cheered again as he lowered himself back down. "I challenge the Loner to a sparring match. Here. In the middle of the city. His brawn versus my brain."

Loner stopped in his tracks. He turned slowly to pay attention to the madman in the middle of the city. This man was out of his mind.

"This demonstration would illustrate the pristine gifts given to us, and to give you hope that we can use these gifts to protect you. We will give you back hope. If I win our sparring match, then the Loner must join me in my quest to serve the people," Franchise preached as he looked into the distance. "But if I lose, I will pay him....oh I don't know.....$50,000 DOLLARS!" he yelled as he erupted into boisterous laughter. "The Loner can't resist competition, and definitely can't refuse money," Franchise chuckled.

Loner froze. $50,000. No way. There was no way. But he had flown in by helicopter. And he did have money signs on his costume. Was it worth the exposure? So much money. It would ease the burden of travel. Speed up the process of finding information. Finding his brother Mateo. Franchise continued to ramble to the reporters as Loner slinked away to a nearby alley and laid his satchel next to a few garbage cans. No one was paying attention to him, they were fixed on the man in the green suit. Good. Nobody would mess with his stuff. He pressed forward, easing past the crowd. If not money, then information. He pushed forward and came to the center edge of the circle. A final second guess. Was the risk worth finding more information on his brother's whereabouts? Yes.

Loner stepped forward into the circle as the crowd fell silent. He cleared his throat which resembled a low growl. Franchise turned with a puzzled looked on his face. Loner was leaning slightly forward with both his arms cocked back.

Franchise took a step forward with his arm outstretched, "Citizen, please step back, I don't wish for you to get hurt if the Loner were to show his ugly mug."

Loner sucked his teeth. "There is no way you can have the money to pay me. So, I require something else."

Franchise's face lit up with joy, "It is you! I can only imagine what you require! Whatever you ask, I can provide it," he said with a flick of his wrist. "I have had my eye on you for a while. We need you."

Loner sucked his teeth again. "The name the news gave me speaks for itself. I do things on my own. Let's call the sparring match a loss for you already, so I can move along."

Franchise's eyes widened, "A loss? For me? AHAHAHAHA, my dear Loner......I promised these people a show!" he shouted with his arms outstretched toward the crowd. "What ELSE did you have in mind," he asked smugly.

"Information," breathed Loner.

"I see," said Franchise, "possibly pertaining to Mateo?" Loner stood straight up and started walking toward Franchise.

"I may know something," sputtered Franchise as he backed up with his arms waving in front of him, "But it would cost that sparring match."

Loner grunted and gave a slight nod. "These people can't be here; they need to get out of this area."

Franchise sighed heavily, "Yeah…I guess you are right...Dear people.….THE MATCH WAS ON!" he blared as he shot back into the air, "For your safety you must get to a safe distance. Once everyone is safe, then we will begin, and THE LONER will join this team to protect you!"

Franchise zipped through the air escorting the crowd down the street. He wasn't particularly fast, nor did he travel very high. As he bumbled through the air, Loner had his eyes fixed on him. The hoses that connected from the backpack to the boots must supply fuel or energy of some kind. And what did the metal dollar sign do? He started scanning his surroundings. All urban. Sides of the street littered with cars and parking meters. Surrounded by tall skyscrapers. The roads had manhole covers every hundred feet or so. Franchise could stay out of reach. How could he close the distance? Franchise finished shuttling people out of harm's way. He seemed eager to begin.

Franchise bumbled up to, and landed, fifty meters away from Loner. The street they occupied was barren, although cheering could be heard in the distance. He walked forward with his arms spread wide at his sides and started, "It doesn't really seem fair." Loner remained silent; maybe he'll ramble and give off something useful. Franchise continued, "That you really don't know anything about me, but I know so much about you." Loner grunted and started to walk slowly towards Franchise. "You have the gift of super strength, and you've had it for fifteen years to practice and master it," babbled Franchise. "You discovered it during high school," he spat.

This was true for Loner. He grew up with normal parents and a normal brother and was never particularly good at anything. His freshman year in high school he tried his hand at sports and joined the wrestling team. He never excelled and was often scoffed at. The coach would actually use him to accept forfeits for the team in the 275-pound weight class. This was a running joke for a long time until his coach misread the match list. One night when Loner went to retrieve a forfeit, there was an opponent waiting for him. His coach willingly let the match begin thinking this would be the final straw to make Loner quit and leave the team. The match began and Loner ducked and dodged his massive opponent. He saw an opening and took a shot under his 275-pound opponent. In a complete moment of terror of being crushed he clutched his opponent's legs and pulled them into his chest. His eyes grew blurry to the point where he could no longer see, and he panicked. He stood up to his feet and threw his arms in the air. Seconds later, his sight returned to see the crowd silent and gawking. His opponent was found lying feet from him, unconscious. He was later told that he picked up and threw his opponent with ease and the boy, twice his size, fell on his head.

Franchise continued his monologue. He seemed impressed with himself and seemed to mimic the mannerisms of the protagonists in movies.

"Your brother was kidnapped, and you ran away from home traveling with a carnival from city to city looking for him. Trying to find any information possible," he stated as a matter of fact.

He had most of the information. But this was a relief that he doesn't know the details. This was general information that could be found in newspapers and articles if someone looked hard enough. Loner felt at ease that Franchise doesn't know more. He doesn't know what happened after the match that night. Loner's mother drove him and his brother home, glorifying the night's victory. When they arrived home, she noticed the front door cracked a few inches open. Sometimes his father would forget to close the door behind him; this was not uncommon. What they found inside, was. In the living room, they found four men, gruff and wearing long trench coats. They were taking turns striking and hitting his father, cursing and shouting. When they caught a glimpse of the rest of the family, they were soon consumed by it as well. Loner's father, through swollen eyes, was instructed that he would now be forced to watch the same punishment continued onto his family. First Loner's mother, then they turned on him. Loner tried to retrace his stepped. Tried to lose his sight, tried to protect his family and himself. But he was beaten badly. He laid there whimpering as he saw the men approach his little brother Mateo. As the man with a metal pipe raised it above his head, Mateo lifted his arms to protect his head and face. The man crashed down full force with the pipe. The pipe seemed to come to life. The closer it came to Mateo's handed, it appeared to split and splash and finally run into his hands. It looked like the bottom of a waterfall as it crashed and flowed, running into his fingertips. Mateo looked up at the men with tears in his eyes, paired with shock and awe. The four men looked at each other in disbelief. Then with a simple nod, one of the men picked up Mateo, slung him over his shoulder screaming. The four men ran out the door. That was the last time Loner saw his brother. Loner was furious with the actions, or lack thereof, that were to come. His father never explained or put any effort into finding his brother. He remained solemn and distant. After two weeks of nothing, Loner left. He threw on a hooded jacket, put a few clothes in a backpack and left.

He traveled for a few weeks looking for anything, any clue of his brother. Fatigued and famished he stumbled upon a traveling carnival. While picking through a garbage can to reminisce about food, he picked up a weathered NOW HIRING sign. His rationale was that he could cover more ground and travel to different places easier while being able to sustain himself. He applied and got a job loading and unloading for the show, while also taking care of the animals. One show, he was backstage waiting for the show to finish so he could start cleaning. One of the horses became spooked and many patrons were in danger of being trampled. Loner ran out in front of the wild horse and scooped it up like a baby or how someone would carry a bride. The audience was in complete shock and didn't know how to react. In a moment's notice, the strong man of the show ran in with gleeful laughter. He introduced Loner to the crowd as the strong man's own son. For years, Loner followed the carnival as the 'Strong man's son' and was raised by him.

The Strong Man was able to help him control and learn how to manipulate his strength. Wallace Westgate, a former polish boxer, and current strongman taught Loner how to focus and maintain posture as well as become proficient at boxing. Years later a fire tore through the carnivals camp consuming most of it to include Wallace. Devastated, Loner left the carnival and continued his search for his brother on his own.

"You may be able to beat me in physical capacity, but you are no match for my mental agility," Franchise scoffed.

With a sneer, he stood straight up, and his eyes became distant for a few seconds. In those few seconds, Franchise was able to step outside of himself. As if looking from above. Everything was cascaded in a dull, cool bluish color. Different aspects of the world were highlighted in vibrant light and instantly drew his attention. From handles on car doors, to the position of the manhole covers. Franchise was taking in all the information surrounding him and categorizing it. This included Loner. He calculated height, weight, and posture. He was capturing every last detail, down to the loosening knot of his left boot lace. But there was something odd. The fact that there was nothing unusual or out of place about him was concerning. Maybe this wasn't the one they call Loner. He appeared normal with no unusual attributes or signs of supernatural capabilities. This did not match the research that he had done.

"Peculiar," Franchise started, "not what I expected."

"Let's get on with it," Loner spat back.

Franchise took a deep breath in and let out a heavy sigh. He bent over and supported most of his weight on his hands, which were placed on his knees and sprung upwards. He shot up with one hand on his hip, and the other fist pointed in front of his face. He hung in the air about six to eight feet. Franchise smirked and reached toward his belt to secure a round disc with a flat dollar sign on it. "Let's see if you live up to all the hype," Franchise said under his breath. He reared back like a professional baseball pitcher, and as his arm shot forward he shouted, "BENJAMIN'S BOLAS!"

With a WWIIIRRRL the disc sailed through the air. Loner sunk his left leg to the rear to brace himself. He didn't know what to expect. Franchise had a smile grow on his face as a loud KURCHLUNK sound echoed through the streets. The center of the disk exploded open, and the two halves were halted by a TWANG as the cable between them caught. The bolas seemed to gain speed as they made contact with Loner's chest. ZZZWWWITHP. The cable sucked his arms into his body and made him hunch forward. Loner straightened his back, took in a breath and flexed. His eyes began to blur as he rolled his shoulders forward, and the cable snapped like an old guitar string. Franchise raised his eyebrows and said to himself, "there he is." He fell back into himself, and the same factors were illuminated, but now Loner was lit up like a Christmas tree. From his head to his boots he was dowsed in a dull, fuzzy blue haze. This haze flowed in waves and pulses. What was literally seconds, Franchise instantly learned everything anatomically about Loner. But it was different now, polar-opposite. Instead of ordinary, this man was brimming with power. He seemed invulnerable, unshakable, with incomparable strength. And then in an instant, there was just grey. There was no more flowing haze. No brimming power. Just normal again.

Loner's sight returned, and he regained focus. He shot his eyes upwards and started to pace towards Franchise. His posture returned as his shoulders rolled forward and his arms tilted backwards. He tilted his head quickly from side to side as a loud cracking sound echoed through the street. He now realized what could be found in the discs on Franchises belt. But what else could be on there? As he walked forward, his eyes flickered from side to side, looking for something that he could us to block or deflect incoming projectiles. He continued to portray an offensive stance, gritting his teeth with his sunglasses over his eyes. He could see the expression that this caused fill Franchise's face.

Confusion still filled Franchise's mind. What had happened to Loner's supernatural gift? Why couldn't he see it now? Why was it only a flicker? He needed more information. He needed to test him more. His hand returned to his belt and retrieved another disk.

With the same motion as before he repeated, "BENJAMIN'S BOLAS!" The disk cut through the air. And just like before, the disk opened with a KURCHLUNK.

Loner waited until the bolas were almost centered on his body. He reached out with his right hand and gripped the door of a nearby car. As he flexed, his eyes dilated, and he effortlessly pulled the door off its hinges, letting screws and scrap metal fall to the ground. In a fluid motion, he blindly threw the car door forward, as if returning a baseball. With a ZZZWWWITHP, the bolas coiled around the car door as it tumbled through the air, end over end, until it punctured the asphalt, and stuck out like a lawn dart.

There it was again. Loner's body beamed with an aura once more. The same dull hue but the chest and arms were painfully bright. It was like looking into the halogen headlights on a car. And as suddenly as it appeared, as soon as Loner placed his hands down to his sides, the highlights were gone. He returned to gray. This was odd. People with gifts, rarities, hidden patterns, and puzzles, were always illuminated. Franchises ability let him see, analyze, and comprehend difficult problems, processes, and situations. But with Loner, it seemed like he was getting a weak signal that kept coming and going. Like a car radio that was passing county lines. He did learn something. Loner targeted different muscle groups. His strength was heightened, but he could apply more to certain areas. This could prove to be problematic. He had anticipated ten times the strength of a normal man. Not more. The equipment he designed wasn't strong enough for this. He had to approach it a different way.

Loner continued to approach the airborne Franchise. While continuing forward, he leaned over and scooped up a single manhole cover. He lined up directly with Franchise, squared off his feet shoulder width apart, took a deep breath in and flexed. He swung the manhole cover up above his head to his other hand and swung it forward like an ax chopping wood. He released it from his fingertips as it raced through the air, mimicking the blade of a table saw. As he regained his sight, he saw panic consume Franchise's face.

Franchise's eyes grew wide. He pointed his toes downward, which looked to engage the boosters on his boots. It wasn't fast enough, and he accepted this fact. He tucked his head and raised his left arm trying to protect his body with the metal sign on his forearm. The manhole cover collided with Franchise, and he tumbled out of the sky, similar to a bumble bee being sprayed by a garden hose. The manhole cover continued to sail through the air, eventually sinking into a parked car. Franchise reacted as most people would after falling eight feet out of the air onto their side. He slowly made it to his feet catching his breath. He breathed heavy with disbelief. Loner continued to approach him. Franchise relaxed his body and let his left arm hang. He reached over with his right hand and pressed something in the middle of the giant dollar sign. The two lines remain in the same place, but the sign itself turned sideways and then the lines sunk down into it.

Loner stopped. "What the fuck?" he muttered.

Franchise raised his left arm, making a fist. He pointed his fist at Loner. Keeping his arm straight, he tilted his wrist and hand towards the ground. THWIP. A soft twanging sound occurred. Loner quickly braced himself and flexed. He felt a quick pressure against his shoulder. He regained his vision to see one of the dollar sign lines tumble away.

"A fucking crossbow," he huffed, "it's a fucking crossbow."

He hunched forward into a three-point stance, flexed, and leapt forward, cocking his fist backwards. Franchise took to the air again, missing Loner barely. Loner landed with his fist pulverizing the ground under him. His back now towards Franchise. Franchise pointed his left arm at Loner, touched the tip of the remaining bolt with his fingertip, and focused. Loner shone vibrant white and blue. He went grey. Franchise tilted his wrist downward. THWIP. As the bolt struck the back of Loner's calf, it erupted into tendrils of electricity. Loner's body seized as he let out a curdling scream. As the electricity fizzled, nothing remained but smoke that billowed from Loner himself.

Nothing was heard over the gentle hiss of the fabric of Loner's pants. The bolt fell to the ground and Loner rose to his feet. No one said a word. Even Franchise had a look of surprise.

Franchise became lost in thought. How could Loner be hurt? Seamlessly invulnerable. Affected by a crossbow bolt? He's not always invulnerable! He could turn it on and off! This changed the game. But how? We need to continue to evaluate. But this took concentration. Focus. It's exhausting.

Loner turned slowly, gritting his teeth. This wasn't good. For so long, he had hidden from plain sight. But now people have seen weakness. This needed to end, quickly. He must assert himself again, to ensure the people still respect his power. He turned fully towards Franchise and took off in a jog, picking up speed.

Franchise remained in place, staying vigilant. Engaging his comprehension. Still nothing, but dull grey. Loner was getting closer and closer, but not super. It's time to get him to back off. Franchise steadied his arm and flipped his wrist. FWIPP FWIPP. Two bolts soared through the air. GRRT. The sound of leather being pulled and stretched tight. Loner's body burst into illumination. The bolts hit Loner, crumpled, and blow into splinters. GRRT, Loner's body faded back to grey.

Loner's eyes regained focus and he continued to advance towards Franchise. He reached out and put his hand on a car door and flexed. GRRT, his eyes dilated, and he tore the door clear off its hinges. GRRT, he let the flex go and regained his sight.

Franchise continued to observe. He watched Loner light up and go dim as he tore the door off. He needed to keep him at bay, so he could gain more information. He loaded two more bolts and touched the tip of one. He aimed at Loner and tilted his wrist. FWIPP, the bolt was met by the car door. As the bolt started to erupt in lightning, GRRT, Loner slung the door forward and released it at Franchise. The door raced towards Franchise as it spun end over end. Franchise's eyes grew wide as he rose higher into the air to avoid the unlikely projectile.

Loner grew tired of the mockery and stupid crossbow. He wanted this to end. He wanted this to end now. The surrounding people do not need to know any more about him than they already do. He needed to close the distance. End this little fight. Find out what Franchise knew.

Patterns, rhythms, and probabilities raced through Franchise's head. His face looked frantic as he tried to learn, comprehend, and defeat his opponent. Loner assumed a forward leaning stance and lunged towards Franchise again. GRRT.

"YAARRR," Loner grunted as he swung in the dark. Franchise evaded ever so slightly again as he lost his train of thought.

As Loner regained his sight, he glared upwards. Franchise was almost overhead. In the center of the sole of his boots appeared to be some sort of gyroscope. Interwoven rings revolving endlessly. Some sort of new technology never seen before. This was how he could propel himself. These needed to be broken.

Loner realized that every time he flexed, Franchise was able to anticipate or react to it. He needed to be able to get close enough to grab at least one boot. Without the boots, he couldn't fly. Without the boots, he would not win. He tested a flex to see if it would get a reaction. GRRT. Franchise recoiled as if he were just startled. He took off further into the air and moved away. Loner took off in a sprint towards him.

Loner was grey again. The blue aura faded away. But he was charging again. Franchise gripped his belt and threw another disk backhanded and screamed, "BENJAMIN'S BOLAS!" He followed this by firing two bolts from his arm.

GRRT. Loner swatted away the disk that then exploded and wrapped up a nearby parking meter. The two bolts struck and exploded into splinters again. He swooped down and ripped another manhole cover out of the ground and hurled it through the air towards Franchise. GRRT. The moment he felt the manhole cover leave his fingertips, he released his flex. He saw the look of panic on Franchise's face again and the direction he looked into to try and escape. GRRT. Loner lunged up and forward in the direction of Franchise. Loner's arms were outstretched with fingers spread. Blind. GRRT. His vision returned to see his fingertips inches away from Franchise's boot. His hand made contact. GRRT. His fist closed as he heard a wiz, crunch, and pop sound. GRRT. He released his hand and regained sight. Loner fell effortlessly to the ground, ready for impact. He watched a panicked Franchise try to compensate.

Unknowing, Franchise tried to engage his boosters to dodge the incoming manhole cover. His only functioning booster engaged and sent him spiraling out of control, unable to compensate. He impacted the ground with a solid thud and skid for a few feet. He slowly clambered, trying to rise again.

This was your chance to show the people force again. This was how you gained the respect back. Loner strode towards Franchise with a quickened pace.

"Say it's over guy," Loner shot out.

Obviously hurt, Franchise clutched his opposite arm, barely able to hold his head up. "No good sir......it's not over....," he sputtered.

Loner stopped a hundred feet away, next to a four-door sedan. GRRT. With effort, he lifted it above his head. The crowd gasped in shock and horror.

"NOOOOOOO!" the young girl screamed as she ran up to grasp Franchise. It was the young girl in purple with her shiny cape.

Suddenly, the car became light, as if Loner wasn't holding it at all. He released his hands, and it appeared the car stayed aloft. GRRT. His vision returned. He was face to face with something. Something unrecognizable. It was bluish and almost transparent. It was mostly round and stout. Not very many identifying features. It had long slender arms that ended in what looked to be fingerless globes for hands. It had some sort of resemblance of a thumb. His hands looked like some sort of child's boxing gloves. His arms connected with its round and bulbous body. Its front was mostly what seemed to be face. Circular vacant eyes and an open gape mouth with two dull teeth on either side. His face was completed with two primitive pointless ears on either side of his head. It had large round feet with no toes that seemed to support its body weight under the large oaf.

Loner stepped back. He was able to see through this thing. It was able to support the weight of the car effortlessly. Still with its vacant stare, it seemed to sigh as if to await instructions. Loner looked back at the girl. She was focused with a determined scowl gripping her face. Her arms were outstretched emitting the same strange bluish color as the creature.

"It's fine Fathom," started Franchise, "put Miles away." Franchise scuttled to his feet. "You win Loner. You have out done me."

Fathom stood, fixed on the monster and Loner. Franchise put his hand on her shoulder and gave her a convincing nod as to say, "It's over." She drew her hands in towards her body, and the monster started to fold into itself in a spiral until it seemed to blow away into the wind. The car fell and struck the ground.

Loner's eyes were fixed on the girl. Whatever that was, was unpredictable. Dangerous. A projection that was able to lift a car like him. He'll have to keep an eye on her and write down his findings. Research to understand. But for now, he needed to get the information on his brother, and disappear. Away from the public. Away from the cameras. Today was enough. Cautiously, he approached the two.

"Tell me what you know so I can leave," Loner huffed.

Franchise gave a heavy sigh. He stared at the ground and gave slight nods while perching his lips. "That was our agreement," he started, "were you aware of a man that goes by the name Boss Winston?"

"Big wig in the crime game. What about it?" Loner questioned.

"His men took your brother," Franchise offered.

Loner stood there fixed. "And what am I supposed to do with that? A man who can never be found. His associates are never caught. Nowhere to start. Just possible hearsay?" Loner shot back at him.

Franchise continued to look disappointed. He grasped at his belt and opened a compartment. He slipped out a piece of paper and offered it to Loner.

"His guys have been roughing people up in these areas. It was much closer than you were fifteen minutes ago."

Loner took the paper, glanced at it for a second, folded it and put it in his pocket. He stepped off and started to walk quickly in the direction that he had placed his bag.

"Loner?" Franchise called. Loner looked over his shoulder to acknowledge. "Would you consider still joining us? You could do a lot of good for this city."

Loner turned back around and started into a jog. No time for games. There was still work to do. This lead might be worth checking out. It had to be. At least enough to expose himself. Should definitely check it out on the way to the job. He snatched up his stuff and took off down an alley. As Loner darted away, the crowd and reporters started swarming in towards Franchise.

"You OK?" Fathom whispered.

"Yes Fathom. I'm Ok." Franchise smiled.

"I don't think he's going to join us," she offered.

"Shut up Fathom," he grumbled.

Reporters surrounded the two and bombarded them with questions. You could only make out every couple of "WHO" or "WHAT" or "HOW."

Franchise struck as much of a superhero pose as he could with his injured arm and responded directly into a camera, "hahaha! A worthy opponent! Not today, but one day, the Loner will join our effort! Let this serve as an invitation to all heroes, for I would still search the country for new members!"

Franchise continued to banter on about helping this dear city, and about heroes for the people. The crowd slowly dissipated until a handful of people remain.

"Could we go yet?" Fathom pried.

"Yes Fathom," Franchise gave in as he pressed the symbol on his belt buckle. CHIWOOP. "Emmitt, come get us, we're ready to go."

Rubble got swept to the sides as the green helicopter dropped into view and lowered a rope ladder. The two climbed up and settled inside. The pilot looked back and gave a gentle nod.

Fathom leaned over to shout in Franchise's ear, "I'm sorry he didn't want to join your team."

"I realize now that challenging one of the world's strongest men was a bad idea," he smiled back. And they both laughed for a bit.

The helicopter approached an almost condemned "U-Store" storage facility. Emmitt landed the helicopter on top, and the three exited, and gave a good stretch on the roof of the building. They enter through the roof and walked down the stairs into the middle of the abandoned storage facility. The facility was relatively baron with only a few pieces of furniture. A few of the storage lockers were rolled up, and there were mattresses and lockers in them. They looked to have been converted into living quarters. In the middle of the facility, there was a large old table with a couple of chairs around it, two couches, and a desk with a computer.

Franchise plopped into his old dusty computer chair. He rubbed his eyes and looked up at his two computer screens. "Next on the list of recruits….Wendell Roberts."

Chapter Two: Franchise

"Next on the list of recruits," he started, "Wendell Roberts."

He whirled around in his chair, his arms outstretched in the air trying to get some acknowledgement.

"He'll make a fine addition. He's another hero with super strength. I've been keeping an eye on him. He'll be a great replacement for Loner in the meantime."

Fathom looked back blankly. She blinked a few times as if searching for something to say. She fought back a yawn. Her eyes widened, and she chirped, "Can I play with Miles?"

Franchise slumped into himself and put his head in his hands. Reluctantly he responded, "Yeah, sure."

She jumped up and squealed. She bowed her head ever so slightly and reached her hands out from her body, palms up, and fingers spread. Small circles of spiraling blue emitted from her hands. Thirty feet away the transparent blue monster spiraled out of nowhere. And there he gawked with his open mouth and a vacant gaze. Fathom leapt out and hugged the beast. She exclaimed, "Miles! I missed you!"

"He did stuff today. That's new." Franchise started.

Fathom put one finger up as in a matter of fact, "Yes. He dances with me." She threw her head to the side with a little bit of attitude.

She put her hands on her hips and Miles quickly followed, imitating each movement. Her hands remained with a dim glow as she fluidly and melodically moved around the floor. Miles followed gracefully. Franchise seemed to peer through as if in a trance.

Analyzing. Fifteen-year-old female. Ability: Conjuration. Able to conjure creature at whim. Mostly small creatures to include mice, rabbits, squirrels, and foxes. Starting to be able to maneuver them through the articulation of hands. The largest of creatures was her imaginary friend Miles. Conjurations did not seem to be able to maneuver or think on their own.

"You OK?" asked Fathom.

"Yeah just glad you're a part of the team," Franchise responded.

"You did get beat up pretty bad," Fathom shot back.

"Shut up Fathom." Franchise said as he became lost in thought. It was only two weeks earlier that he had found her. Through his research he found a child causing a disturbance at an orphanage. He arrived in his full suit and knocked several times. When the door opened he began, "Hello Ma'am, my name was Franchise…"

"HURRY, this way!" The woman cut him off. She dragged him down the hallway by his arm. He was pulled into a large room with bunk beds crammed into it. In the corner of the room was Miles. A small girl with her back towards the door was hugging him and seemed to be trying to protect him. All the other children in the room surrounded them.

"You have to get her out of here," the woman started, "I knew there was something wrong with her. And yesterday! That thing! You have to take her out of here! She just doesn't belong!"

"What's wrong with her?" Franchise asked confused.

"Are you fucking serious?" She shot back trying to keep it under her breath. "Ever since she got here, she never fit in. She never interacted with anyone. And then animals! Everywhere! Small blue animals. The ledges, inside, outside, fucking everywhere. And then yesterday, this fucking thing!"

"Absolutely. Amazing," Franchise said in awe. He found himself lost in thought.

This poor girl. She was feeling outcast and all alone. She had no one to talk to. Or even to be her friend. So, she created one. She's not bad. She's not wrong. There was nothing wrong with her. She's a scared child with an imaginary friend. You could just see hers.

Fathom continued to clutch Miles as the other boys and girls taunted her.

"Eww, look at it."

"It looks so dumb."

"What is that?"

"Gross!"

"Stop it! Leave him alone!" Fathom cried.

Franchise kept his voice low as he asked, "What is going to happen to the girl?"

"If you don't take her, I'm going to give her to the first people who do," she quickly responded.

His face was shocked. Then concerned. He then appeared to have just figured something out or solved a puzzle and was pleased with himself.

"I'll take her," he started, "and make a sizable donation to your orphanage."

She tackled him with a hug and screamed, "Thank you!"

"On one condition." Franchise started with his head tilted and eyebrows raised. She nodded as to tell him to continue.

He continued, "I need everything on her; records, files, pictures, addresses, names, everything. Every last scrap of paper you have. Every last bit of evidence that she was ever here is destroyed. When she leaves with me, she never existed here."

The women looked taken aback. He walked past her. And pushed his way through the taunting kids. He kneeled next to the sobbing girl. He stretched out one hand and started, "Hello young hero." She looked over her shoulder and gave a small smile.

"You have been chosen to help keep your city safe. You have been chosen because of your wonderful gift. Together we can help keep other people safe. Everyone will see how amazing you are and praise your name for all of your help."

She turned around and looked up at him with tears in her eyes. She turned and grabbed his hand while still holding on to one of Miles'.

Franchise spoke directly to her in a low voice. "For now, until we get to our new home, you have to put him away. People don't understand like I do. They are scared because they do not understand.

But when we get home, he can come out whenever you want." He said it with a smile, but it was met with tears. She looked at Miles with tears filling her eyes. She turned her hand, so her palm was facing the ground and closed her hand into a fist. Miles slowly crumpled into himself and faded away.

A little later, Franchise was looking down at a file with a picture of Fathom paper clipped to it. There were so many ruffled pieces of paper rattled throughout it. But only a first name "Piper" could be found through all of it. He shut the file with one hand. He looked over to Fathom and said, "Let's get you home."

She replied, "Where do you live?"

"I just bought a place. It's a bit of a fixer upper. But its home just the same."

Fathom looked concerned and avoided eye contact. She pried, "Are you different too?"

He responded, "Yes young hero, I am. But please, don't call me mister. I am Franchise, hero of this city."

As they walked down the street, she inquired once again, "What can you do?"

Franchise looked puzzled and couldn't find the best way to interpret it to a child. "Mine is hard to explain," he said with a smile, "I can think really well."

She looked back with a blank stare and responded, "That's not special."

Franchise stopped baffled. He tried to piece together an answer. "No, I um…hmm.. I am able to figure things out quickly."

"How do you use it?" she asked.

He took a knee to try to make her understand on her level. "Imagine a puzzle with thousands of pieces. It might take normal people hours to sort through and build only the border. If I concentrate hard enough, I can figure out where all the pieces go in seconds."

"Oh," she looked satisfied with that answer and then continued, "why are you dressed like that?"

He took a second. Sucked on his teeth and then responded, "Well, I am Franchise. A Franchise is a lucrative business. That's why I have the money signs on me. And that is why my colors are green and gold."

"That has nothing to do with your power," Fathom questioned, "Why don't you have a question mark on you?"

Franchise was clearly becoming more and more frustrated, "It's a dollar sign. Because I have lots of money."

Fathom interrogated, "How'd you get so much money?"

"HUUNNNGGG," Franchise growled as he turned and took a knee facing her, "I used my gift to solve a very important puzzle and the prize for winning was a lot of money."

"Oh," she seemed satisfied with that response until, "What was the puzzle?"

"It was a puzzle with numbers."

"Like a math puzzle?"

"Not really a math puzzle."

"Like a Soo-Doe-Coo puzzle?"

"No, not a Sudoku puzzle."

"I don't get it."

Franchise put his head in his hands and spat out, "The stock market, I used it to play the stock market!"

"What's the stock market?" asked Fathom.

He responded in frustration, "It's where businesses put all their money, and I figured out the trends on how to use it and I made a lot of money!"

She stopped in her tracks and cried in distress, "You cheated!"

He stopped and raised his eyebrows. He slowly lowered to one knee to make eye contact. "I am not using the money for personal gain. I am using it to make the world better. There would be people using the same money to make life harder for people. And I am using it to protect them."

She gave a nod. He returned to his feet, and they continued to walk. Later on, she responded, "You still cheated." Franchise threw his hands into the air as if to symbolize giving up.

Franchise finally came back from his daydream. He spoke out loud but only to himself, "How do I get Wendell?"

Emmitt responded, "Why don'tcha challenge him to a fight?"

"Shut up Emmitt." Franchise shot back. He whirled around in his chair again and stated, "Look, all the research I did on Loner said that he'd respect strength. He only tends to show himself if someone is about to get hurt or there is some sort of reward. I took a gamble. I lost. So, sue me."

He whirled back around toward his computer screen as his face lit up. He thought to himself. Wendell was different. He knew he was different. And he kept it hidden. He was a big contributor to his community. He and his neighborhood were pretty bad off. But he contributed consistently to be a positive role model. He was the kind of hero we need.

He stood up from his chair and stretched upwards. "Tomorrow. First thing, we're going to his neighborhood."

Early the next morning Franchise and Fathom headed out on foot. It was only a few miles away; there was no need to run the copter. Plus seeing costumed heroes on patrol would be good publicity. They turned onto the overcrowded street. It seemed that the apartments were literally stacked on top of each other just to squeeze more people into them. Children were in the streets riding bikes, darting through traffic. The older kids were playing basketball with a dinged-up rim with no net. Franchise saw him in the distance. There was a slender yet tall black man, roughly 23 years of age. He was helping an elderly couple out of their vehicle and unloading their groceries for them. As they approached him, Wendell shook hands with the old man. They were both smiling, revealing Wendell's missing front tooth and remaining yellow teeth. He turned his head to catch Franchise and Fathom out of the corner of his eye. The smile left his face and concern filled it.

"Mr. Roberts," Franchise called outstretching his hand, "it is a pleasure to meet you."

The old couple slunk off, keeping their eyes on the two costumed people.

"Mr. Roberts, I am Franchise."

Wendell cocked an eyebrow and responded, "Ain't you the one fighting the other guy on TV?"

Franchise raised both eyebrows and responded embarrassedly, "that would be me." He continued regaining his composure, "But I am not here to talk about that. I am here to talk to you about an opportunity!" In a low voice, he offered, "I understand you can do some pretty impressive things."

Franchise fell into the back of his mind as his field of view became a low glow.

Analyzing: Wendell Roberts. 23 years old male. 185 LBS. Super strength: Lower extremities only. Heightened speed, super jumping capabilities.

Wendell's concern showed through his face. "What'd you mean?"

Franchise took a deep breath, rolled his shoulders back, and began using his best superhero monologue stance, "Wendell, I have done my research. I am looking for people like us to change the world. There are people out there willing to hurt others, take advantage of others, and simply put, just do bad things. I want to help those in need. You have a gift, Wendell. You learned of it in high school, no? Basketball, if I remember correctly. During a game, you jumped from half court and made a dunk." Franchise tilted his head downward and pulled his goggles down far enough to look over the top of them. "You could have played in college. Probably professionally as well. If you didn't drop out of high school. I understand why. You did it, so you could help your family. Help raise the kids in the community. That's why you stuck around? To keep them safe and keep an eye out for them, huh?"

Wendell's face shifted from concern to almost relief, mixed with guilt.

"And this was why we need you," Franchise started again, putting his hand on Wendell's shoulder, "you have a good heart and want to help. I want you and your gift to help people everywhere."

Wendell nudged, "Come with you where?"

"Wherever we are needed young hero," Franchise responded with a smile.

"I couldn't leave these people, they need me. These kids need a role model, or they go bad. Plus, how'd I know you ain't pulling my leg?" Wendell asked with a skeptical look on his face.

A smirk grew on Franchise's face. "Well, this is Fathom. Go ahead Fathom… introduce our new friend to Miles."

Fathom gave a slight nod and outstretched her handed. As Miles came into view, Wendell's mouth dropped in awe.

Franchise continued, "And as for your neighborhood. I am willing to make an anonymous, sizable donation to the schools. Build a park with functioning equipment. Clean up the streets and create a better environment for the kids in it." Wendell seemed amused by this offer. Franchise continued, "Now sir, we've shown you what we can do. How about you show us what ten years of practice can do. Let's see if I was right about you."

Wendell looked down, as if he was contemplating. He turned to face the building behind him. Six floors of windows towered over the group. Still looking at his shoes, he gave a few slight nods. He crouched down into a squat. He looked at the top of the building. Then a loud CRUNCH echoed down the street. The concrete sidewalk where he was standing was smashed into a hundred pieces. He launched into the air. He kept his eyes closed. It seemed that he enjoyed the wind whipping by him. Kind of like a dog with its head out the window. As he approached the top of the building, he was losing momentum. He reached out with his hands and grabbed the ledge, pulling himself on top.

Franchise pointed his arm upward and made a fist. With a quick flick, the gyroscopes in his boots engaged and propelled him upwards. He stopped face level with Wendell. He outstretched his hand and asked, "So I guess you accept my offer? You're joining the team?"

Wendell nodded and gave a firm hand shake in agreeance.

"You're going to need a costume," Franchise chuckled.

Back at U- Store, Franchise walked Wendell down a hallway with open lockers. "Pick one that doesn't already have stuff in it, and it's yours. Once you're settled in, come find me and we can figure out the details." Wendell gave a quick nod. Franchise walked off, leaving the room. Fathom stepped up next to Wendell. She pried, "So how do you do it?"

"Do what?" he shrugged.

"For me, I close my eyes, and I think really hard. I think about what I want to see. When my hand's tingle, I open my eyes. What I imagine was in front of me." As she explained, she demonstrated by summoning Miles.

Wendell laughs, "Mine's a lot easier then that. Mine's more like a flex. I think about it, give it a push, and it happens."

Fathom looked confused, "So you're not strong all the time?"

"Nope, just when I want."

She answered, "But why not all the time?"

"I'll show you. Make a muscle." He demonstrated by flexing his arm.

She cooperated and flexed her bicep. "Now hold it," he encouraged, "Come on now, go on, hold it."

She looked exhausted and finally released with a "Whew."

"That's why," Wendell chuckled.

The two walked into the main lobby. Fathom asked, "What do you want your name to be?"

Wendell shrugged his shoulders. Franchise whirled around in his chair with his arms up, "What about 'The incredible jumping man'?"

Wendell cocked an eyebrow with a short, "no," followed by, "Couldn't I just go by Super Wendell?" That was met with a resounding No from Franchise.

"Oooh, I know!" Fathom interjected. She looked proud of herself. "You jump really good and high like a grasshopper!"

"Grasshopper?" Wendell repeated.

Franchise was taken aback as if he had just discovered something. "That's really good. Oh, the costume possibilities!"

"I don't like it," said Wendell shaking his head.

"But I came up with it," Fathom said with a whimper.

Franchise continued to talk to himself, "Yeah it could be yellowish orange, or with brown…"

Wendell became defensive, "But grasshoppers just…ugh, are puny and…people usually squish 'em, and …..There aren't even any in the city!"

"There could be….one," Fathom shot back, pointing with a smirk.

Franchise prattled on, "OH, and I could make a backpack with 'wings' so he could control his fall…" Franchise started grasping at papers on the desk and began scribbling frantically.

Wendell turned towards Franchise and complained, "Come on mayne, it's like the second name we came up with."

Fathom under her breath, "I came up with it."

Franchise stood up immediately and turned the paper around, "From this day forth! You are known as….!"

Days later Franchise helped Wendell put on his suit. He took great care explaining the pieces. Most of the suit was orange and brown with purple highlights. There were patches over the shoulders, forearms, and thighs that were striped and made of thick protective pads. The headpiece was made up mostly of a mask that protected the eyes.

"This was my favorite part!" Franchise chuckled as he helped Wendell into the backpack. The backpack was flat against the back and curved in a dome shape.

"If you press the 'H' on your straps on your chest you'll deploy the wings. They're strong enough to support your weight. After you rocket yourself into the air, you can stretch your wings to either slow your decent or glide for short distances. Then hit the 'H' again and retract them."

Wendell looked at himself in a full-length mirror. "Alright, I could work with this." He hit the 'H' on his chest. With a SHHUR-CHUNK the wings sprung open. "These are pretty cool too."

Franchise fell into his computer chair looking accomplished. "I am glad you like them. Welcome to the team…Hopper."

Franchise then lost himself staring at the two computer screens. On the left, a woman named Madalyn McCray. On the right, a teenage boy named Ripley Greggers.

Chapter Three: Loner

Loner sat on top of a hill looking down on a building. It was surrounded with a chain link fence topped with barbed wire. One portion seemed to have been knocked down. The sun was setting as he sat down against a tree. He needed to make sure no one else was around. He'll read through his notes again and watch for a while. He opened his bag and took out a ragged file. It had scraps of paper and sheets scattered throughout. On the outside of the folder was a giant red stamp that read CLASSIFIED.

He flipped it open to the front few pages. He flipped past the cover sheets marked with the Logo "SYNERGY CO." He came upon a file marked Experiment #289 Codename: Meat. He began to read through it again, for the hundredth time. He had to make sure. This file was hard to follow for most of it was journal entries. From what he had gathered, SYNERGY was engineering weapons. Kind of. SYNERGY was trying to replicate individuals with abilities. Trying to take subjects and imbue abilities onto them. Multiple subjects had similar tests and trials applied to them with varying results.

Some resulted in creatures like Meat. SYNERGY was trying to create and replicate the power of endurance and regeneration. Trying to find the recipe to create Soldiers who never fatigued and that weren't susceptible to disease or physical ailments. One of the partially successful experiments was codenamed Meat. The stats on this guy were impressive. Loner gathered from the notes that this thing was at least 8 feet tall, probably pushing 400LBS. Solid muscle. But incapable of independent thought. Or so the company thought. There was an explosion at Synergy that allowed numerous experiments to escape. To include the bumbling mass that was Meat. Two weeks ago, Loner was approached by a man who went by the name of Dr. Monroe. A scientist that worked for SYNERGY CO. Apparently SYNERGY had been following Loner for some time because of what he was capable of. Dr. Monroe offered Loner a job. Some of the experiments were easy to regain, but others were well past the capabilities of SYNERGY outside of their confinement. In return for tracking down some of these potentially hazardous experiments, and preparing them for capture, he, in turn, would be compensated financially as well as afforded resources to help find his brother. Loner wasn't fond of the idea of an organization that created monsters. But he liked the idea of monsters on the loose a lot less. The lesser of two evils was evident. This organization obviously had resources and outlandish capabilities. What would happen if he refused? He accepted the offer. For now. He'd complete this one job, gain from it, and make a better-informed decision later on. Getting a monster off the streets was not going to harm anyone. For now, he would be making progress towards finding his brother.

He sat watching this building. No activity. The downed fence was the easiest way in. That's probably how this thing got in. He went over the facts again. Giant monster, not smart, resistant to fatigue. So, he'd enter, look around, try to confine the beast. Then call SYNERGY for pick up. Sounded simple on paper. But nothing ever goes to plan. He took his bag and placed it next to the tree. Tucked all of his documents and his sunglasses inside. He headed down the hill cautiously. As he approached the downed fence, he noticed dark black circles leading to the building. Footprints? They didn't resemble feet. They were crusted. He leaned down to touch one. It reeked of iron. Was this blood? Were these puddles of blood? Loner didn't like the looks of this. He followed the trail through one of the doors to the building. There were dim lights flickering on and off. It was cold.

Almost like a freezer. This place was once a facility that made medications. But why did it feel like a slaughterhouse? He continued to follow the marks on the floor. The stench started to become overwhelming. Iron. Almost like stale blood. Unsettling. As he continued through the hallways, the marks started to look different. He crouched down to touch one again. This one was wet. He brought it up to his nose. It was blood and it's clotting. Not fresh. But not old either. Was it eating something? What does an eight foot, four-hundred-pound monster eat? Probably whatever it wanted. He pushed on down the hallway. He started to see his breath. It got colder. He stopped. He heard breathing. Heavy, labored breathing. He approached the sound slowly with caution. The doors to a medical freezer were torn off and thrown on the floor. There was smeared blood all over the sides. The heavy breathing echoed from within the freezer. Loner halted. It was hard to see. He started to slowly move to the side, trying to peer into the freezer. In the corner, there was a giant dark spot. He could see the back of it rise and fell. It seemed to be crouched in the corner. Just sitting there, breathing. There didn't seem to be anyone around, nobody injured. Loner had to find out what was going on. What this thing was. He picked up some scrap metal on the ground and hugged the wall, trying to stay in the shadows. He took the scrap and threw it across the room. As it collided with another metal door, it resounded with a loud metallic KLANG.

The shape in the freezer gave another deep breath, and then rose. It was still crouched in the freezer as it turned. It seemed to shuffle. Maybe the thing was injured? It shuffled to the entrance of the freezer and ducked to avoid hitting the top of the doorway. Through the moments of flickering light, Loner was able to see…this thing. It stood upright and shuttled forward slowly. It towered over Loner. It was a massive incarnation that looked roughly human. But it's skin. There was no skin. It was all just muscle tissue that seemed to ooze and drip. It had no face. Just more tissue. There were sunken in places where eyes should be, and a gape for a mouth. It drew in another deep, labored breath. Its head appeared to connect to its mass of shoulders and its arms ended in what looked like large, clumsy five-fingered hands. Those prints were foot prints. Kind of. But what was it doing?

The name was appropriate. Meat. A giant hulking goliath of muscle. A cold environment made sense. So, he won't spoil, or bleed out? But what now? Giant monster. How to package this thing up for Monroe? We'll figure that out in a minute. The monster stared off into the distance for a few minutes then turned and shambled back into the freezer. Loner carefully worked his way back out of the building and to his bag. He rummaged through it and found a small cell phone. He picked it up and pressed the send button. There was a click.

"I found the thing," Loner started. He rattled off the location of the building and continued, "You sending a truck or what?"

The voice on the other end spoke, "Standby."

"What do you want me to do with this thing?" asked Loner.

As the words fell out of his mouth, three fifteen passenger vans pulled up to the outside of the gate. Loner hung up the phone. Men poured out of the vans in SWAT suits, all carrying firearms. A fourth vehicle followed up the rear. It resembled an armored vehicle for a bank. The men flooded the gate and started to pull security around the facility. One of the men approached Loner. The man was donned from head to toe in black SWAT gear. The only deviation was a white symbol in the top left corner of his vest. It was a white and black, back to back triangles with a large "S" in one and a "C" in the other.

The man barked, "Where is #289?"

Loner pointed at the door. "I found it in there. It's held up in a freezer."

The man barked back, "You need to bring it to us."

"You guys got the weapons. You go grab that thing," Loner shot back.

The man scowled, "I would not risk my men, that was why you were hired. Freak. To grab the Freak. You want payment? You will go grab #289 and bring it to us. Once it is out here, we will contain it."

Loner sucked his teeth, "Freak huh?" He stepped forward until he was nose to nose with the guard. The man didn't budge. Loner sucked his teeth again and started towards the door. He entered, once again following the footprints.

"HEY!" he yelled, "MEAT FACE." Loner wasn't happy. He tended to throw caution to the wind when he got mad.

"Come on you fucking meatbag. Come out of your hidey hole and follow me out of this place. So, Captain Dickbag can taser your skinless face off."

Still no sight of it. Loner rounded the corner and was face to face with it. It loomed outside of the freezer door. More menacing now that he was face to face with it.

"PSST. HEY. Come on meatbag, let's go." Loner clapped his hands. It just stood there, breathing with a vacant gaze.

"I really don't want to touch you," Loner mumbled to himself.

Loner slowly approached the monstrosity. It tilted its head slightly up several times as if it was a dog sniffing the air. Loner stopped in his tacks. This probably was not a good idea. Meat quickly turned and faced Loner. It arched its back and reached its arms outwards and let out an ear-piercing garbled roar, "GGGRRRRAAWWWLLL."

"Fuck," Loner hissed. He rocked back and forth a few quick times breathing in and out quickly to psych himself up. "Alright…we're going in."

GRRT. He flexed and pushed off his back foot and launched towards the monster. He had his left hand out in front of him as a guide and his right clenched in a fist behind his head. Unable to see with his eyes dilated; this was the best way to "connect." His left hand made contact with a wet mass. He unloaded his right hand. KRRAAAWKP. GRRT. His vision returned to see the monster barely stumble and catch its balance. It soaked it up. A lot of it. He looked at his fist. Covered in blood from the monster. He looked down; his clothes were also splattered. He looked up in time to saw Meat twisting his trunk and unloading a backhand. GRRT. CRACK. GRRT. Loner connected with the wall. He peered over his shoulder to see the stone wall cracked and broken. This thing hit hard. And took its lumps like a champ. I definitely don't want to be in arms reach. He's got more reach then I do. He made his way back towards the hallway. Meat stood and breathed heavily.

"Come on meat bag, follow me…let's go…"

Slowly it turned and started to head back towards the freezer.

"Fuck man. Knock out drag out. Take you to taser town."

Loner flexed, GRRT, and launched forward again. He made contact and clung to it. He used his right leg to locate its "knee" and took a deep breath and kicked downward. KRRRK. "GRAAAWWWL," the beast bellowed as it fell to its knees. Loner reached up with his right arm and grabbed what felt like under its head and tried to reach under its left arm with his. He started driving his heels down dragging this slimy, massive meat monster as it flailed, trying to rise back to its feet.

Loners arms started to shake, "Alright big fella….gotta take a break."

GRRT. His vision returned as he released the beast and gave some space. He frantically looked around to ensure he was going the right direction. The monster stumbled to its feet and turned.

Loner thought to himself, "We got a long way to go Meaty. I can't hold on for that long."

Meat swiped downward at Loner with a bellow. Then attempted a backhand again. Loner continued to avoid contact with the blows.

"That's the ticket, keep it coming." Meat lunged with another downwards swipe.

GRRT. Loner reached out with his left and dug his fingers into meaty, sticky flesh. He dragged it across his body and landed another right hook into the monster. GRRT. Alright, his back was towards us. Loner lunged with another flex and dug both hands into the monsters back. Taking one step back at a time and then jerking the monster back. Loner started to make headway as he began to tremble again. GRRT. He let go. He peered behind him again. Light, we're almost there. His head was screaming. A blinding headache was creeping through his temples. His kidneys began to ache. A couple more times he thought. Then Captain Dickbag could fuck with him. He backed up, and the monster turned around. "GRRAAAWWWL," it rumbled. Loner could hear chattering in the distance. Meat swung his tremendous arms towards Loner. GRRT. He put his hands up to catch. THUMMP. Loner's back hit the wall. As he pushed back against the massive arms. He felt himself sink into the concrete wall. His temples began to throb. Suddenly, a giant baseball glove shaped hand grasped around his face. He couldn't breathe. He pushed back and sunk into the wall more. He started to panic. He grabbed at the mitt with his left and started to lay into it with his right. TWACK. TWACK. TWACK. As the mitt opened for a second, he gasped for air. His body started to shake. He put both feet against the monster and thrust backwards. He launched himself through the side of the building. He landed hard. GRRT.

"HUNGGGHG," he gasped for air as his vision returned.

The monster could be seen through the hole in the side of the building. He scanned the faces of the surprised men in riot gear. He found Captain Dickbag. Loner gestured towards the monster with both palms facing upwards and gestured, "hengh?"

Captain Dickbag shook his head "no" and pointed to the center of the fenced area.

Loner grumbled. Meat had turned itself around and began to shamble back inside. Loner took off in a jog. GRRT. He collided with the beast. He started jerking the monster back, while driving his heels in. He heard the men shout and yell. He didn't care. He felt the breeze and knew he's outside. The monster continued to flail and produce guttural growls. GRRT. He let go and back peddled until he fell backwards. Ringing in his ears got louder and louder as his vision returned. His head was screaming, and his sides felt like they were splitting. He looked up and saw the team jump into action. It was as if you put a wounded insect onto an ant hill. The men respectively shoot the monster with taser rounds until it continued to seize on the ground. Four men come around the side of it and hose it down with what looked like smoke or fog.

As it lifted, parts of Meat were frozen. Loner smirked, "Liquid nitro huh?"

After several more minutes, another team removed a large box from the armored vehicle. Put Meat in it, locked it, and sealed it in the armored vehicle.

"Get up," barked Captain Dickbag. Loner made his way back to his feet. The man continued, "Dr. Monroe wants to speak with you. You are coming with us."

Loner didn't like this very much. "Let me grab my things," he scoffed.

He didn't know what to really think. His head was killing him, and his sides felt like they were going to burst open. He recovered his items and was ushered into the back of one of the vehicles with a few armed guards. He rode in the back, massaging his temples. Flexing took a toll. Flexing caused his adrenal glands to work overtime and produce such a state in his body to where he had supernatural strength and near invulnerability. But with such an increased amount, also came all the other side effects. The dilated pupils, screaming headaches, pain in the kidneys. He laid his head on the side of the vehicle and held his sides for comfort. He began to drift off with the gentle vibrations of the car. He came back to when the vehicle came to a stop. He opened his eyes as the back door swung open. He seemed to be inside some sort of garage. It was huge with fleets of vehicles. He watched the armored vehicle drive through a giant gate as two massive doors shut and locked behind it. Captain Dickbag came into view and gave a wave to signal to exit the vehicle. Loner cracked his neck to the side and tried to push the pain away. At least to the back of his head for now. He had to pay attention. He didn't know where he was, or who was here. The captain turned and started walking through the garage. Loner followed. As they approached a door that needed key card access, Loner saw something out of the corner of his eye. He turned towards them. They kind of looked like robots. One was welding some piece of machinery. Another was open. Someone could fit inside. Another man walked up to and backed into it. He seemed to press a few buttons, and the suit closed around him. The outside of the suit looked to come alive as it stood up from a slump. The machine methodically paced over to a section of pallets with what looked like more machine parts. It picked it up with ease and began to maneuver it around.

Loner questioned the Captain, "If ya'll have those things. Why'd ya'll get me?"

The captain replied shortly, "We work for the doctor, not the Engineer."

"The Engineer?" Loner asked.

The captain ignored Loner as he beeped through the door. He escorted Loner through a couple of corridors. They came upon an empty room with no door. There was a cabinet, a bed, a bin near the door, and bathroom with a shower.

"There is a change of clothes in the cabinet. If you leave your clothes in the bin, they will be cleaned. For now, rest. Dr. Monroe will send for you later," the captain looked for some acknowledgement.

Loner pursed his lips and gave a slight nod. The captain turned and left the room. Loner still didn't like him. He also didn't know what to think of this place. Hordes of people, or soldiers, or men in metal suits. Giant facility with a massive garage. What else was here? What else was going on here? He looked down at his clothes. They were caked with dried and clotted blood. It smelt terrible.

"They better not fuck my shit up," he said to himself.

As he was taking off his jacket, he peered out the door. There was no one, not a single person walking around, or talking. The entire hallway appeared to be empty. He continued to undress and throw his garments in the bin by the door. He entered the bathroom and turned on the shower. There was no mirror in the bathroom. He betted he looked terrible. As he stepped into the shower, the hot water stung as it hit small cuts. Probably from the walls he was thrown into. Or through. Not completely invulnerable. He felt himself drifting off as the heat penetrated his skin. His body ached, and his head still throbbed. But these were the consequences for straining his body. He opened his eyes. He felt he's been standing there for at least an hour. He grabbed a towel and wrapped himself in it. He shuffled to the closet and found plain white clothes and a pair of slip on shoes. He got dressed and then grabbed his bag, looking into the bin. His clothes were already gone. He sat on the bed and pulled a notebook out of his bag, flipping to a clear page. Past his notes about Franchise and the girl who could make a monster. He drew the Synergy symbol. And then started writing about his encounter with the Meat monster. With his final entry, he felt himself drifting off again.

KNOCK. KNOCK. There was a rap on the doorway. Loner opened his eyes. His notebook was flayed open on his chest. He must have passed out. He blinked a few times and looked to see who was there. It was an older gentleman, late forties or early fifties. He wore large gold rimmed bi-focals that covered most of his face and sat upon his large and bulbous nose. He had one of those faces where his chin seemed to fall back and connected with his neck. His hands were tucked neatly into the pockets of his lab jacket.

"Loner, once you get dressed, meet me down the hall," Dr. Monroe pointed to the top of the bin.

Then he turned and shuttled out of view. Loner rose and gave a stern stretch. Still really stiff. Headache was still there but had gotten a little better. He gathered his clothes and inspected them. They looked like they did prior to the engagement. All the blood was gone. He got dressed, then threw his notes into his bag. He slung his bag over his shoulder and placed his glasses on top of his head. He started off in the direction Dr. Monroe had walked and found himself in what looked to be a large conference room and Dr. Monroe looking at a clipboard. There was a large table in the middle of the room between them. In front of the chair nearest to Loner, there was a manila folder with a small rectangle on top of it.

"You aided in the capture of Meat. I hope it wasn't too difficult for you?" the Doctor started as he scowled at his clipboard, flipping back and forth through the contents. He gestured for Loner to sit at the table. He continued, "As agreed upon, I have provided what you were promised. The card on top is your financial resources. Swipe it and any amount within reason will automatically be approved. In the folder are police reports on your brother."

Loner slipped the card into his pocket and flipped open the folder.

The Doctor continued, "For ten years all reports that matched the description of your brother. The bottom line, since his disappearance, he has not been found alive or dead."

Loner threw the folder onto the table, "That's it? That's all of it?"

"No. But that is all of it for now. That proves that he was never found. As he aged, he changed appearance. We have the technology to create an image that would likely resemble him now."

"Then do it!" Loner barked.

"That could be payment for your next assignment," the doctor responded coldly. "In addition, you can keep the card while continuing to work for us."

Loner grumbled, "More monsters?"

"Yes," the doctor confirmed, "this one could be more hostile though."

"Why not put your super squad in the rock'em sock'em suits and round up these creeps yourself?" Loner pried.

The doctor shot back a confused looked.

Loner continued, "Metal suits. People forklifts, I saw them in the garage."

"That is not a resource available to me," the doctor said emotionlessly, "would you like more intelligence on your brother's whereabouts?"

Loner gritted his teeth. Don't really feel like getting the taser treatment. Also, really don't want to wrestle a bloody meat monster again. "Show me what you got."

The doctor took another folder attached to his clipboard and slid it across the table. The label read: #445 Gorge. Loner looked up through the tops of his eyes and asked, "What's a Gorge?"

The doctor turned his back to Loner and began, "Gorge was an experiment testing the boundaries of metabolism."

Loner cocked an eyebrow and scrunched his face.

"One again the purpose was to engineer weapons that could continue to sustain and fight with limited resources," the Doctor continued.

"Still not following why you need me to find a monster that could diet."

The doctor was not amused. He continued, "The experiment seemed to take rather well to the treatment. Much like certain animals, like the snake, it can sustain itself for a little more than a week with one meal. When testing its limits in seeing how long it could sustain, it seemed to regress as a human. Becoming an emaciated husk. We started to feed it again. Much like the reptiles, once it reached a certain weight or threshold, it began to molt and develop again."

Loner looked puzzled, "Wait. If you starved it, it became a shriveled monster. And if you keep feeding it would become human again. If you keep feeding it, it'd become a monster again?"

"Precisely. Consequently, once it hit a certain threshold, it would grow and become less human. Through trials and tests, we found this threshold was roughly its body weight at the time."

"Once it eats its body weight it grows?" Loner asked.

"It doubles in size." The doctor told Loner, his face becoming concerned. The doctor continued, "The first few times were quite insignificant. But you could imagine once it got larger. Not only did it increase in size, but strength and endurance as well."

"Explain…" Loner started as he put his hand over his face in frustration, "what it turned into…"

"It depends," the doctor quipped.

Loner peered through his fingers, "Depends on what?

"What it has consumed. It takes on the attributes of its prey. Tactically, it's marvelous. This allows it to track and apprehend more of its prey in its habitat. We tried various food sources with a wide variety of results from birds to reptiles." It was as if the doctor respected its capabilities.

"I don't think I want to know where you guys found it now," Loner said with resentment.

"A slaughterhouse," the doctor said plainly.

"You want me to track down, and capture a bloodthirsty, carnivorous, cow beast?" Loner asked sarcastically.

"Yes."

"Yee, haw," Loner muttered as he stood and gathered his things. "I'll need a couple of days."

The doctor gave a nod of acknowledgement.

Loner's favorite Captain arrived at the door and escorted him out of the building. Loner looked over his shoulder and started walking towards the addresses that Franchise had scribbled on his list.

Still in the conference room, Dr. Monroe approached a wall intercom and held down the button. "Mr. Winston," he started, "we need to talk about the Loner."

The box cracked and responded, "Come to the 'Balcony' Doctor. The Engineer has something to show us."

Chapter Four: Doctor Monroe

He released his finger from the box. Incompetent hack. The Engineer. Stealing praise and accomplishments for less than adequate work. Doctor Monroe was a scientist. He worked with flesh and bone. He pushed the limits of the human capability to try to produce a true masterpiece of potential. The Engineer tried to accomplish the same with machines and machinations. That's not where the answers were hidden. Hundreds of examples to show for his work. The answer was in the genetics. He had found this through tireless and exact research. And this Engineer dared to corrupt his findings with metal and wires.

Not everyone had the potential. Certain people could acquire, possess, carry, use, or resist extraordinary talents. Once this was identified, far less subjects failed to yield results. Now this hack was using my findings to "create" new weapons. Bah. He was only sought after for his own ability. A supernatural with the ability of articulation. Through his clockwork brain, he could comprehend and construct "wonders." To be honest, this facility was a testament to his practical application. His disgust came when this Engineer crept into his territory, altering and improving the human form. Prior to his discovery of superior application, he was crudely attaching machinations to people to enable "warriors." Savage. Beneath the genius of a doctor. Science would triumph over technology. He would prove it to Winston. Winston was the enabler. He had sought out the Doctor and funded his research. Not only funded but fully supplied it. It was through his connections that he procured so many "compliant" subjects.

Boss Winston was incredibly connected throughout the city. His connection with the prison warden was extremely beneficially. Genius. Death row inmates. Using fake injections and carting them off here. Genius. Sure, if the testing didn't yield results, then termination of fodder for the other experiments was more than necessary.

Dr. Monroe continued to get lost in his thoughts as he shuffled to the 'Balcony'. The Balcony was a windowed bridge that overlooked a jail block. There was protectant glass that shielded the viewers and allowed full visibility. This was normally where the experiments were set loose to gauge limitations or lack thereof. Testing of the new creations was important to understand, replicate, or avoid the same techniques or procedures. Initially, they were tested on the mechanically stitched together horror warriors. But they were soon outclassed by superior creations. Dr. Monroe chuckled at the thought.

As he stepped onto the balcony, he saw Boss Winston standing in the middle leaning against the barrier. He was a tall and weathered man. He wore his usual ankle length trench coat and matching formal hat. It was something you would expect from an old-timey detective. His face was scarred. It was the only exposed portion of his skin. On the other side of the balcony, there was a shorter, slender man walking up to meet them. He had a shaved head and steely grey eyes. His face was blank as if it was made of stone. He wore blue jeans and a stained undershirt. He carried a briefcase in his right hand.

"As dapper as ever Engineer," Dr. Monroe jutted.

"Insignificant babble," he scoffed back.

"Gentlemen," Boss Winston interrupted, "enough with the greetings of the day. We have business to attend to." His voice was low and gruff like a midwestern cowboy. "It seems the Engineer has branched out from your discovery of receptive genes," he said to Doctor Monroe.

"And what did he attempt to do with it? Attach razorblades to house cats again?" he scoffed.

"I plan to implant alterations," the Engineer said coldly, "applications should take effect immediately."

The doctor laughed from his gut, "My work speaks for itself. It takes time. Lots of time. Altering genes. Application. Alteration. Months. Stringent methods. And I have evidence the easier methods involve breeding and starting from scratch. PAH! You wish to create one instantly! Impossible! You and your lust for technology! Leave creating the perfect being to me!"

The Engineer showed no emotion. "Let's give the man a chance. After all, he's done wonders with my building," offered Boss Winston.

"Humor me, magician!" Dr. Monroe laughed, "Explain your home-schooled theories to me."

The Engineer turned to the balcony and placed the briefcase on top of it. With a click, it swung open. Inside were five octagons. Each had different symbols struck on them.

"Toys?" Doctor Monroe offered.

The Engineer turned to face the others. "Hopefully you are familiar with your own research, clown." Dr. Monroe scrunched his face in disapproval.

The Engineer continued, "Elemental capabilities are limited to five. The same as the points of the pentagram: Earth, Fire, Water, Air, and Spirit. In this application, we know that spirit pertains to the manipulation of electricity. There are different variations and applications and intensities. You, clown, figured out how to identify who could foster these types of applications. I have manufactured a means to apply them. A vehicle or an applicator, if you would."

Boss Winston perked up. "Instant weapons?" he asked.

"If applied to receptive hosts, yes," he answered.

"Hog wash!" Dr. Monroe spat. "If this was even fathomable, why elemental application? Elements have proven volatile. Why not apply simpler tasks like strength for your first science fair?"

"I could match any of your abominations with any of my amplification technology. Simple. My men maneuver this fortress with ease whereas you lose your brute and hire vagabond street trash errand boys to find them," the Engineer fired back.

"HRRUMPH," Boss Winston cleared his throat, "I am also interested towards the choice Engineer."

"Machinations require a power source. Cars and generators are easy. But controlling elements is more difficult. Manipulating water requires a tank, a pump, and energy source which become clumsy and impractical. If the source was actually able to be the power source they wouldn't need the other components. They would already contain them."

"And how do you propose to 'introduce' this catalyst into the receiving host," pried Dr. Monroe.

The Engineer reached into the box and pulled out a single octagon. "Placed at the base of the neck. When engaged, the device injects the catalyst fibers up, down, and throughout the spinal column. They fuse and become part of the subject's anatomy. If the host has the perspective traits, when the catalyst is introduced, the two fuse, and the host should be able to use their hidden gift, instantaneously."

"And say if it's a total failure, and it explodes?" Doctor Monroe jested.

"Then it would give me means to test the new 'medic' protocol in the amplification suits," the Engineer quipped back.

"Medic protocol?" asked Boss Winston.

"The suit initiates medical treatment to the user that is already inside or climbs inside. Once it is fully operational, it will be revolutionary for warfare. Wounded and battered climbing into suits.

As they close into it, the suit will seal bullet holes, seal up amputations, and start lifesaving interventions so the user could continue to fight," the Engineer explained.

"That would be remarkable Engineer," applauded Boss Winston.

"I agree," said the Engineer.

"In theory," shot Dr. Monroe, "since all of this was just ideas and worthless conversation."

"Could we see it?" asked Boss Winston.

The Engineer gave a nod and started pressing buttons on a device he had on his arm. One of his workers appeared at the end of the balcony in one of his amplification suits. The Engineer walked the octagon down to him. They talked for a minute, then the worker gave a nod and disappeared into the hallway. The Engineer walked back to stand with the others. The three watched as two workers dragged out an inmate dressed in an orange jumpsuit. They couldn't hear clearly on the balcony, but it seemed he was screaming and begging. They always do. The two workers struck the inmate down to his knees and held him there by his arms. A third worker appeared in the doorway of the cell block. He walked over to the other two, then handed over the octagon and appeared to be giving the others explanation. He returned to the doorway and pressed a few buttons on the suit. It opened, and the worker climbed out. He walked back through the door that then shut behind him.

"Leaving the suit unmanned?" asked Boss Winston.

"In case the protocol is needed," replied the Engineer.

"So what failure elemental abomination do we get the pleasure of witnessing today," taunted Dr. Monroe.

"This device unleashes the power of wind," the Engineer responded. He pressed a few buttons on his wrist device and spoke into it. "Do it."

One of the workers took the octagon and placed it at the base of the screaming man's neck. He pressed a few buttons and forcefully pushed down on the device. Instantly the man writhed in pain to the point of uncontrollable convulsions. The three watched as the man screamed and twitched uncontrollably. The two workers continued to restrain the man until he seemed to slip through their hands. His skin started to shred into finer and finer pieces. The workers let go of the man and started to back up. The man started to contort and fold upon himself giving guttural screams and pleas. His skin continued to shred and started to swirl around where he was injected. It started to vortex in and out. He was unrecognizable now. He roughly maintained the shape of a man, but was made almost completely of vortexing tunnels, like a shambling scarecrow made of small tornadoes. His movements were unpredictable and random. From standing up, back to being hunched over as if he was glitching. Suddenly he turned towards the two workers in the room. WHIIRRLLLL. The air in the room started to circulate and whip around. There was pressure on the glass that protected the three men on the Balcony. Boss Winston leaned in, intent on how the experiment was unfolding. The two workers continued to back pedal as one began to hit buttons on his suit in an attempt to communicate to someone. The prisoner slowly pointed one of his whirling arms in the direction of the workers. The prisoner started to tilt its trunk, and then it fired off a whipping vortex towards the workers. One worker was hit and soared through the air. CRACK. He impacted the side of the cell block. The rest of the prisoners' body filtered through the vortex where it re-formed at the end. The worker tried to rise from the ground. The prisoner placed both of its hands onto the worker. Pieces of the suit were being spiraled off as if it was being hit with a drill. The prisoner rolled back what used to be its shoulders and threw both of his arms forward. Both vortexing arms ripped through the worker and hit the wall behind him. The prisoner held its stance as the whipping arms began to grow outward. This completely pushed the rest of the worker's body apart. Pieces of the unsuspecting worker flew in all directions. They started to circle around the room with the whirling wind.

Boss Winston stood fixed on the nightmare in front of him. This hurricane man was remarkable. The Engineer spent as much time watching the gruesome act as he did typing on his device. Dr. Monroe fell into the back of his mind. He thought to himself, "The hack actually did it. He created a delivery system to introduce the catalyst. And created a person….made of wind."

The other worker in the cell block ran to the door. Frantically pressing buttons to escape the fate of the other worker. The prisoner continued to move uncontrollably back and forth. It moved as if it were made of TV static. He blinked in and out of sight and got closer and closer to the remaining worker. The whirlwind inside the cell block continued to increase. The prisoner reached the remaining worker and placed one of its funnel arms onto the suit. It appeared that it was pressing through the seams and cracks into the suit. The worker started to tremble and seize wildly, making uncontrollable movements like the prisoner.

"He's scrambling him inside the suit!" Doctor Monroe exclaimed. The prisoner reclaimed his funnel arm from the suit as the suit opened, and whoever was in it poured out onto the floor. With no one inside the room, the prisoner began to whip through the cell block with screams of agony.

Dr. Monroe looked at the Engineer, and with panic in his voice, he asked, "How are you going to contain it? It seems uncontrollable. If it can writhe through a suit, what if it figures out it can slip through the vents and…"

At that moment, the Engineer pressed a few buttons on his wrist device and spoke into it. His voice resounded through out the cell block. "Prisoner, near the entrance of the room you will find an unused suit. If you can climb into it, I can ease your suffering."

The wind monster, that was once the prisoner, whirled through the cell block with a resounding RAWLLLL. The pressure continued to build against the barrier on the balcony. "Engineer, I hope you have a plan," Boss Winston said calmly.

The Engineer stood with his eyes fixed on the cell block. He punched a few more buttons on his wrist device. Suddenly, inside the remaining suit, lights began to flash. The monster turned suddenly and lunged forward in a whirlwind. As it collided with the suit, the Engineer's fingers flew across his device. The suit shut around the creature. It tried to escape through the cracks and seams. It appeared to be sucked back in. A resounding FFICKTOCK echoed throughout the cell block. "Grab the suit and bring it to my lab now," the Engineer stated firmly into his device. The door to the block opened, and four workers entered and dragged the other suit out. It was rattling back and forth with the wind monster trapped inside.

"What the…how?" asked Dr. Monroe.

"Vacuum. For now. It exceeded my calculations. I must make adjustments." He turned and walked briskly off the Balcony. Boss Winston gave a chuckle as he turned to a shaken Dr. Monroe. "Said we had to talk about something earlier?"

The doctor blinked a few times and then shook his head. "Yes, Loner. He retrieved one of the experiments."

"And?" Boss Winston asked annoyed.

"He wasn't satisfied with the information he received."

"Then give him 'better' information next time," Boss Winston said, still annoyed. "Did he get bugged?"

"Yes Sir, there are tracking devices in all of his clothing. We also gathered vital information on his capabilities."

"Could you replicate it yet?"

"No, not yet."

Boss Winston sucked his teeth. "Let's wander on down to the Engineer's lab and find out how he's handling our latest discovery."

Doctor Monroe gave a slight nod, put his hands in his pockets and lead the way. The two walked up to the doors of the workshop and the doors slid open. On one side, there was a large glass looking capsule that contained a whirlwind.

"What's the verdict, Engineer?" Boss Winston called out.

The Engineer was also in some sort of suit. It was larger than the worker's suits. But it had no front to it. He sat against the back of it and used a combination of levers, buttons, and joysticks to maneuver. He remained focused as the suit continued to complete tasks frantically.

"Could we still use it?" Boss Winston asked again firmly.

"Yes," the Engineer responded shortly.

There were so many moving parts in his workshop. With smoke and a steam hiss, a tank opened beside the Engineer. Inside there was most of one of his suits. Its arms were completed down to the forearms. The Engineer whirled around it, replacing parts and working diligently.

He started sputtering out answers as he worked, "on its own. Won't work. It couldn't. Too unpredictable. Couldn't control. On this. It was a failure." He continued to zip and drill and rivet at the machine. "But paired with one of my devices. It would contain him. With the medic protocol, it should make him comprehendible. If not, at least in the suit, he would be controllable."

He picked up the suit he was working on and moved it against the wall. He then plugged it into his main computer. The suit was similar to the other suits but had some serious modifications. The helmet was no longer removable; it connected to the chest plate and arms which ended at the forearms. The end of the forearms were now completed with caps. The abdomen was clear but covered with some sort of see through material, it connected to the legs that were solid mechanics. He pressed a few buttons on his computer and the visor where the eyes should be, lit up on the suit. The Engineer walked over to the capsule containing the transformed prisoner. He lifted it with the hands of the large suit and walked it back to his newest contraption. He attached the capsule to the wall and mashed a few new buttons. The torrent was sucked into the wall and replaced into the abdomen of the new creation. It writhed back and forth. With a furrowed brow, the Engineer frivolously typed at his keyboard. The machination stopped shuttering.

"Although the initial test for my applicator did not produce practical results, I was still able to harness the pure power it provides." He pressed a few more buttons and spirals of wind poured out of his creations forearm ports and formed what looked to be hands. He pushed a few more buttons and they retracted. "Give me time, and it should be able to act independently. In the meantime, I can control it manually."

"Good work Engineer," Boss Winston praised.

"I would alter the other applicators prior to continuing these trials again. I do not wish to repeat these findings," the Engineer said, lost in his computer screens.

Boss Winston gave a nod and a small laugh. He looked at Doctor Monroe and said, "He brought me a breakthrough. A hurricane machine. And potential elemental weapons at our fingertips. And what do you bring me? Complaints and anxiety over a snoop. I thought you were a little smarter than that doctor."

The doctor looked displeased as if he was just disciplined.

Boss Winston continued, "If you keep giving a duck bread crumbs, it will keep coming back for more."

"But aren't you afraid he'll be able to connect the…" the Doctor started.

"No, and neither should you. Continue to make your breakthroughs. For now, gather as much information as possible. And continue to try and replicate the full body superior strength. No more of this partial body bumpkas you've churned out in the past," Boss Winston said smugly as his fixed the hat upon his head and turned for the door. His trench coat flared with the turn which made for a dramatic exit.

The doctor threw his hands back into his pockets. He kept his head down while he made his way back to his laboratory. His internal conflict continued to rage as he continued to think to himself.

"Bah, the metal head has out done himself today. Outclassed my creations. But only for today. With Meat back in lockdown, he'll serve multiple purposes. Especially once the remaining experiments are recovered. There is no need to go back to the drawing board. Only need is to refine the amazing accomplishments we have already conquered. That should be good enough to earn the praise and respect that this pure genius deserves. Unless," he trailed off.

Unless he could use the application system to introduce the complex strains he's been working. Complex genetic codes. Not to increase or decrease, but to manipulate or alter the material. This would surely gain the respect back. He arrived at his laboratory. It was a much different scene from the Engineer's workshop. Instead of buzzing and clicking of machines and flashing lights, it was a very somber place. Analytic codes covered whiteboards, computers were sparse and orderly. Tabletops were full of beakers and vials. In the corner of the room, there was a double door that loud thuds echoed from. That's where the restrained experiments reside. A life's work. Each created in the desire to manufacture powerful weapons. For the highest bidder.

The thuds made it hard for him to concentrate. He gave a short sigh of frustration and continued his shuffle toward his hallway of accomplishments. He hit the keypad on the wall, and the doors swung open. Giant containers lined the long hallway. Each filled with creatures and projects. Mostly subdued. The thuds come from the end of the hallway. He continued his shuffle through his trophy room.

"I see you finally thawed out," he jeered as he passed Meat's container.

He stopped at the culprit's container as its resident slammed against the glass again.

Doctor Monroe looked at the chart attached to the container and replied, "You don't prefer your new accommodations....Ripley Greggers?" He replaced the clipboard next to the Marking: #2876 BUG.

Chapter Five: Loner

He's done walking around the city. He had made a couple of rounds through the blocks identified in Franchise's scribbles. He found that walking around and ease dropping normally provided the most reliable information. People love to complain. Good, bad, indifferent. It didn't matter; a lot of people love misfortune and loved to complain about it. He perused 'watering holes' and heavily populated areas to see if there had been any disturbances like the ones Franchise described. While there, there was nothing to note. Until a few gripes became similar. Small business owners had been visited by 'investors'. People hung up all their 'dirty laundry' in the street to anybody who would listen to gain sympathy or status. This could be worth losing a day to investigate. Especially if it brought him closer to finding his brother. He looped around and ended his gallivant at the local library.

Loner liked the Library. It was quiet, calm, and he could soak up some of the air conditioning while he did some research. He'd rather read through a few newspapers and walk around instead of fighting another monstrosity. It had been two days since the encounter with Meat and his was still rather sore.

He walked up to one of the people sitting behind the counter. "Excuse me Ma'am," he started, "could you point me in the direction of the newspapers?"

She looked confused, "We don't carry newspapers anymore. Everything's online," she pointed to a cluster of computers sitting against a wall.

He scrunched his face in disapproval. He hated computers. They were so complicated. Unlike this generation, he spent most of his time growing up either with the traveling circus or wandering through cities and states looking for his brother. He walked over and sat at this alien device. He sat for a minute and observed how other people were using the computers. They made it look effortless and elegant. He grabbed the mouse and jiggled it from side to side. The desk top booted up and spread across the screen. It had foreign icons riddled throughout it. He clicked on one and a box popped up on the screen. He hit the 'X', and it disappeared. He clicked on a different icon and yielded a similar result. He grumbled as he stood up and returned to the desk.

"Could you help me?" He asked the distracted women at the desk.

"What do you need help with?" she asked.

"Help me find the newspapers on the computer," he said plainly.

She furrowed her brow and tilted her head to the side. "Which newspaper do you need?" she responded.

He stood there and looked at her. He thought it best not to disclose that he was trying to find if there was criminal activity in the area and of what nature. Or that he was trying to find patterns of conduct of one of the most detrimental crime empires to date. That may raise too many questions and get the attention of people he didn't want around.

She rolled her eyes and pushed back from the desk. She walked over to the computers and Loner followed. She wiggled the mouse, clicked on an icon, and her fingers flew across the key board. Suddenly, there was a rectangle on the screen with a blinking line at the beginning of it.

"Here, this is a search engine. Type whatever you're looking for in there and press enter. You'll get a bunch of things related to it pop up," she instructed and then walked back to her chair.

He sat down and looked at the screen. And then back at the keyboard. And back up at the blinking line. He wished there was newspapers. He used his pointer finger to strike each key. After he hit a key, he looked up to see if it translated onto the screen. He wished there was newspapers. After the time consuming task was done, he pressed the enter button. The screen went white and then filled with blue lines of text. He clicked on one and started to read. He wished there was newspapers.

Hours went by. He'd find a little bit of useful information and scratched it into his notes. He discovered there was an arrow button that he only had to click in order to return to his search. The lady at the desk wasn't happy to have to come show him that. After six hours of sifting through the internet, his eyes burned. He thought he had enough information. He was hungry. He thanked the woman at the counter and was met with a half-hearted smile. He walked down the street to a small diner, walked inside and sat down. He ordered a sandwich and opened his notes to review. There was some legitimacy to the information that Franchise provided. In this area, there were more and more assaults on small business owners. Apparently, the "company" that gave these business holders loans had come back to collect the debts. Familiar story. These loan sharks were rumored to be affiliated with Boss Winston. A really bad character. A ruthless crime Boss. But mostly just a name used as a scare tactic. Nobody had "seen" him before. Or if they did, they gave different descriptions of what he looked like. He continued to look at his notes. He followed up with a list of small business owners and people who worked with this company for loans. There were still a few that hadn't been visited, so he figured he'd start there talking to those people. Today was pretty productive. The check came for his food, and he handed over his card he had received from Doctor Monroe. It was handy. Made life a lot easier. He had even rented a room in town to crash and leave his things in. Hopefully, his detour for his personal vendetta wasn't being tracked by his questionable employer. Hopefully, he could get a few answers prior to boxing a man eating cow monster.

One of the small business owners on the list lived near his hotel. He decided to swing by and ask a few questions about his relationship with them, who they were, and if he had been paid a visit lately. He was exhausted. Physically, mentally, and emotionally exhausted. It was the shred of hope of being reunited with his brother that kept him going. Finally, something to show for years of effort. But walking cleared his head and let him decompress. After some time walking, he had finally arrived at the apartment complex. He pressed the button for the corresponding apartment. He wondered out loud, "what kind of name is Barnaby Finkle?"

"Hello?" buzzed the intercom.

Loner paused for a second. "Eh, yeah, I'm your new neighbor. Just moved in, but I forgot my keys inside. You're the first one to answer; can you do me a favor and let me in please?"

There was hesitation in his voice, "Uh…yeah …hold on."

Easy enough, guy lets him in, he'll follow him to his apartment, and ask some questions. Done this a hundred times. Loner stood there for roughly ten minutes. A metallic click got his attention. The door swung open. Loner grabbed it and with a smile said, "Thanks boss."

A small rotund man with glasses met him. He had thinning hair and seemed to be out of breath. He gave a slight nod. He turned and started to walk away. Loner stepped into the building, stuck his hands in his pockets and slowly followed after the man. He opened the elevator and stepped inside. Loner followed. Side by side, the elevator doors shut.

Loner offered out his hand, "Stanley." It was met half-heartedly with a pudgy hand. With a labored breath he responded, "Barnaby." Loner let a minute go past. Before the door opened, he asked, "What do you do Barnaby?"

The door slid open. Barnaby took a heavy breath in and started to waddle out. "I'm an optometrist."

"Oh, that's cool. You don't hear that every day. You own your own practice?" He offered, trying to keep the conversation going.

It was met with a short lived, "Yeah."

"You go in on it all on your own, or you split it with a partner?" He tried again.

Barnaby gave a slightly annoyed looked over his shoulder and answered, "Nope, just me."

They arrived at Barnaby's apartment, and he started to insert his key into the lock. Loner was still standing behind him. Barnaby looked at him concerned.

Loner asked, "I left my phone in my apartment too. Would it be possible to use your bathroom and phone for a minute? Try to get ahold of a locksmith?"

Barnaby gave a resistant sigh and nodded his head. He was sweating profusely, so sweat splattered everywhere. They enter his apartment. It was dark and stale. There were containers of takeout scattered everywhere. Books stacked on top of papers. The only light was the blue glow of the television that was left on.

Barnaby pointed and said, "Down the hall on the right." Loner gave a quick smile and a nod.

He took off through the cave-ish environment, being careful not to knock over any piles on his way. He reached the bathroom; it was as unkempt as the rest of the apartment. He closed the door and sat down for a minute.

Suddenly there was loud banging coming from the living room. A short pause and then a few more sharp pounds at the door.

"Open up Barnaby," a thick northern accent pierced through the door, "it's your ol' pal, Clint." Loner heard scrambling at the door, it sounded like the chain lock being slid into the door.

"Uhuhuh…One second…," Barnaby stuttered. Loner stood up and crept to the bathroom door. He cracked it open and peered out. The round man finally slipped the lock on, and cautiously opened the door, "Hello Clint--" Barnaby started as the door swung open and was sharply caught by the chain.

"Come on now Barnaby, is this how you treat an ol' pal," he said through gritted teeth as the smile left his face, "Open. The. Door."

"I know I'm late," Barnaby plead, "but, but, but the interest, it it it, raised so suddenly, I need more time."

"Open. The. Door. Barnaby." He echoed.

"Just just just, a few more days," Barnaby stuttered.

The man at the door turned and muttered a few words to people behind him. "Last chance Barnaby." He stared at him for a second and then shrugged his shoulder, "Alright then. Let's invite ourselves in boys."

Clint stepped aside, and a larger Samoan man stepped forward. He gave a quick breath in, then drew in his leg and discharged it into the door. The chain lock busted out of the wall, and the door swung open with a crash, knocking Barnaby to the floor. The Samoan man and another grungy shorter thug scrambled in and snatched up

Barnaby by his arms. Barnaby started stammering incoherent words, trying to spit something out. Clint entered through the broken door way, and he was followed by two fairly muscular men who split in two different directions.

"You know what to do boys," Clint said over his shoulders. The two men start tossing the apartment. Knocking over piles and tearing out drawers.

"Geeze, Barnaby. This place is a wreck," he said with a chuckle. "Now, you owe us money. Do you have it?"

"Nananananoanano," Barnaby stammered.

"You know what that means, right there pal?" Clint said with a smirk. He turned to the men holding his arms. "Let him know how upset we are fellas."

He turned into the kitchen. The Samoan grabbed Barnaby and held both him arms behind his back. The smaller grunt started to lob punches into the round man.

Clint was walking through the kitchen, opening drawers and dumping the contents on the ground. "I'm disappointed, Barnaby. My boss, out of the goodness of his heart, gave you his hard-earned monies. So that you could open your little…um…uh…what was it that you do again you fat fuck?"

Barnaby couldn't acknowledge through the barrage of punches. He whimpered as he was struck again. Clint continued as he rummaged through another drawer, "Loss for words huh? What was it that you do again. Oh yeah, eyes!"

Clint turned his head to the side as he found something. He ducked down and returned to view with a hammer in his hand. Barnaby fell to his knees, and the Samoan threw him to the ground. His back was to the open door. He was sobbing uncontrollably. Clint came around the corner, scraping the hammer across the wall.

"You see buddy, if I don't come back with the money. Well…haha, I'm really going to get an earful. I'm going to have to explain why you couldn't pay. And make sure that you were very, very, very sorry. You eye guys; you use your hands, right?" Barnaby squinted upwards in fear. Clint continued, "You do the…which is better?…1? Or 2? thing right?" he chuckled as he imitated it by flipping the hammer.

Barnaby was crying uncontrollably until his eyes caught sight of Loner. He stopped immediately. Loner stepped through the doorway with his pointer finger up to his lips. Clint continued, "Good boy Barnaby. Take your licks like a man and have the money next time. Right ol' boy?" Barnaby quivered and gave a quick nod as tears filled his eyes again.

Clint raised the hammer above his head. Loner sprinted from the bathroom. He grabbed the hammer by the handle. Clint looked behind him shocked, "What th--?"

GRRT. Loner squeezed the handle and it exploded into splinters. With both hands, he shoved Clint. GRRT. His vision returned as Clint flew over Barnaby, through the open door. At that moment, the other four men in the room turned towards him. Loner slid his leg backwards and took a defensive stance. The short, squat henchmen lunged toward Loner, unloading a cocked fist. Loner took a step back and unloaded an uppercut into his jaw. His teeth clacked together as he fell forward onto his face. These guys were normal joes. A powered-up punch would take their heads clean off. Good thing he still knew how to box. At least this way he could still see. He turned to watch as the other three drew their pistols. He sighed in his head. Maybe he would have to flex. The Samoan squared up and raised his pistol. As he gritted his teeth and started to grunt, Loner reached in the direction of the pistol and lunged. GRRT. The room went dark. He heard the discharge of the pistol. The world lit up from the flash. He covered his eyes with his other arm. The pain in his eyes was excruciating due to the light and his dilated eyes. He felt small pushes against his skin in three different places. The bullets made contact. His hand made contact. He hoped it was the gun. He closed his hand on whatever was in his grip. There was a loud crunch and a pop. The Samoan man screamed in agony. GRRT. He released for a second to catch sight of his surroundings. The Samoan man hit a knee and rolled to his side screaming in pain. It was his arm, not the gun. The force crushed through the bone and popped the flesh of his hand open like a tube of toothpaste. His insides popped out through his palm. He quickly looked in the direction of the other two men. They were wide-eyed as they glanced at each other. They both raised their pistols. Loner lunged in their direction. GRRT. He heard the discharge and covered his eyes. After the sound, he took both his arms and stretched them out to his side to try and catch one or both. He sprinted forward. He made contact. GRRT. He opened his eye to see a large hole in the wall in front of him. Only one man remained in the room. The scared thug trembled as his dropped his pistol. He ran towards the door. Loner took a quick look at the hole in the wall, didn't see the other guy in the next apartment, and he scuttled after the runner. Through the door, he couldn't saw the runner. But on the ground, clutching his ribs, was Clint.

Clint was screaming into his phone, "There's a fucking super here! Send the Terror-cane before the…"

Loner grabbed the phone and pulverized it in a quick flex. He grabbed Clint by the collar of his shirt and pulled him up to face level.

In a low and controlled voice, Loner started, "Who do you work for?" Clint's fear slowly subsided into a smirk as he spat in Loner's face.

GRRT. Loner threw him with a backhand, and he broke through the wall behind him, back into Barnaby's apartment. Clint sputtered and coughed on his own blood as Loner stepped over the rubble to get to him. Loner looked down at the broken shambles of a man. "Who do you work for?" Loner repeated. Clint gurgled on the blood in his mouth and spat, "The Boss."

"Which boss?" Loner interrogated.

Clint gurgled through a chuckle and coughed out, "The bad one."

Loner stepped on his hand as Clint wailed in agony, "WINSTON!"

"The imaginary crime Boss?" Loner shot back.

"Oh, …he's real," Clint sputtered as he attempted to roll to his side. Loner kicked his shoulder, and he landed flat on his back.

"What's a Terror-cane?" Loner asked.

"Oh, Terror-cane?" Clint chuckled again, "You'll see soon enough."

Loner ground the toe of his shoe into Clint's hand again. Clint screamed and choked on his spit. After he caught his breath he began, "Terror-cane is a sup…." His head snapped backwards as a bullet entered through his chin.

Loner's eyes snapped into the direction the bullet came from. In the distance knelt the Samoan with smoke still billowing from the muzzle of the pistol. Loner squared up and stepped off in his direction. The Samoan smirked as he pressed the muzzle under his chin.

Loner lunged. There was a flash and a snap. The Samoan hit the ground. Loner stood over him as the Samoan leaked over the floor.

Loner looked around, over his shoulder. This was a mess. Not really an improvement from earlier. He looked around again.

He put one hand to his mouth and called out, "Barnaby?" A closet door slid open slowly, and the rotund man waddled out. He continued, "You need to get out of here. You have someplace to go?"

Barnaby muttered, "Thank you."

Loner urged, "Barnaby, you need to get out of here. Grab what you need and go."

"Go where? The only other place is my practice."

"I don't care. But if they found you here, they can probably find you there," Loner said plainly as he surveyed the room.

"You saved me," Barnaby said in awe, "How could I repay you?"

Loner was getting frustrated. He rubbed his eyes. They hurt from the exposure to the gun flash. He started, "Nothing I don't need anything, you need to..." He stopped in mid-sentence. "A pair of glasses." Barnaby looked at him blankly.

Loner asked, "Could you make a set of glasses?"

Barnaby looked confused and answered with a, "Yeah, uh, sure we'd have to go to my practice."

Loner responded, "We have to go now. Grab what you need from here because you probably don't want to come back."

Barnaby looked a little star struck as he took a minute, gave a few nods, then started pacing around picking up a few items. Loner stood in the middle of the room. It was only moments before people would start rushing in to see what all the commotion was about. Definitely don't need police. Barnaby was still klutzing around.

"BARNABY!" growled Loner. Barnaby sprung up like a terrified prairie dog. Loner lowered his voice, "It is time to go."

Barnaby gave a few quick nods and with the things clutched in his hands he exits his demolished apartment. Loner stuck very close to him.

"Is it in walking distance?" Loner questioned.

"Eh, what?" Barnaby responded still in a haze

Loner spun him around and held him by the shoulders. "Barnaby, your practice. Is it within walking distance?"

Barnaby just stared back. Even if it was, he didn't look like he'll make it. "Do you have a car?" Loner tried. Barnaby nodded. "Take me to it." Barnaby scuttled along until they came to his vehicle. It must be at least twenty years old. Unfortunately, it was in the same condition as his apartment. Loner ran over to the passenger side, opened the door, scooped the trash out of the seat into the street, and climbed in. Barnaby squeezed into the driver seat, fixed the mirror, then put on his seatbelt. He checked the mirror again, then put the key in the ignition.

"BARNABY!" Loner growled again. He started the car in a hurry.

Within a few minutes, they had arrived at his practice. It actually looked very nice on the outside. They exited the vehicle and Loner followed behind as Barnaby scuttled up to the door. The inside was just as pristine as the outside. They walked to a back room, and Barnaby offered a chair to Loner.

He approached the counter and stopped suddenly and asked, "Why do you need glasses?"

Loner sucked his teeth, "Can you make sunglasses?"

"But you have sunglasses," Barnaby offered as if he was trying to help.

Loner put his head in his hands and let out a long breath. "Prescription. Sunglasses."

"But you don't wear normal glasses…."

Loner took a deep breath and stood. He walked over and grabbed Barnaby's face with both hands. He started nodding his head as he spoke.

"I need special glasses." It was met with a nod. "They need to be sunglasses." It was met with another nod. "When I punch people through walls, my eyes dilate." Another nod. "When my eyes dilate, I can't see." Another nod. "When I punch people through walls, I want to see." Another nod. "Barnaby. Make me glasses so I can see when my eyes are dilated." Another nod. "As many as you can make."

Barnaby crinkled his face, "Why?"

Loner put his head back in his hands, "Because I'm pretty sure I'm going to break a few pairs, Barnaby," he said with resent.

That apparently was good enough for Barnaby as he gave a final nod and escorted Loner back to the chair. He went through his exam thoroughly and competently. Loner was even a little impressed.

"Grinding them will take me an hour," Barnaby offered.

"Any way you could speed that up?" Loner asked. Barnaby shook his head no. Loner gave a nod and followed him into the back where Barnaby started to work.

"What next?" Barnaby asked.

"About what?" Loner queried.

"Where am I going to go? Where am I going to live?" whimpered Barnaby. Loner shook his head.

"Once you're done, this place won't be safe either," Loner clarified.

"Then where?" said Barnaby. He didn't look up from his work, but his expression showed all over his face.

Loner stood, "Look guy. You got in bed with the wrong guys. And by dumb luck, I walked into your life today. And you're not beaten to death with a hammer."

"You could've stopped them earlier," Barnaby shot back looking out the corner of his eye with a smirk on his face.

Loner smirked back. This blubbering tool bag had been through enough. There was no need to play the tough guy. Especially since he was actually helping him. Good people were hard to come by these days.

"You got a computer I could use?" Loner asked. Barnaby pointed over his shoulder. "Let me get your phone," Loner demanded. Barnaby handed it over and returned to his work.

Loner followed his directions into what looked like his office. It was absolutely trashed. This was the Barnaby he knew. He sat in front of the computer screen and wiggled the mouse. His old enemy. The computer.

He found the search engine by walking through his steps earlier that day. He found the phone number to a hotel out of town. He called and reserved a room for two weeks. When they asked for payment, he read off the numbers from his SYNERGY card. The cheery individual on the other end of the phone replied with a chipper, "Thank you sir, we'll see you later!" It took much longer then he thought. He stood up and gave a big stretch before returning to Barnaby. He entered the room to see two sets of glasses sitting on the table and another in Barnaby's hands being polished. Loner placed a set on his face. He couldn't see a thing. GRRT. The world slowly came into focus. Barnaby did it. The fat, sweaty optometrist did it. GRRT. He placed that pair on top of his head and put the other two in his bag.

"Thanks," Loner started, "get everything you need out of this place. I got something for you."

Barnaby scrunched his face and started scuttling around again. Loner left him to his own devices for a few moments. He went to the bathroom and closed the door behind him. What was the damage today? He lifted his shirt. He had purple welts over his chest, arms, and stomach.

"Better than the alternative," he said to himself. The bullets must have connected as soon as he started the flex. Being able to see was going to be so much more convenient.

Suddenly there was a giant crash. The sound of crushing glass echoed through the building. Loner turned out the light and peaked out the door. There was a commotion in the front of the building. Loner slowly crept to where he had last seen Barnaby.

Someone shouted from the front of the building, "Hey now. Y'all in trouble now. We got da Terror-cane wit us dis time. HAHA!"

There was a muffled conversation from several people in the front. Loner slinked to the back, crouching. It must have been the guy that got away. Looked like he found replacement henchmen too.

"WOOOO! TERROR-CANE!" the henchman called through the building.

Loner saw his little fat man cowering in a corner. He swiftly ran up to him. "Is there a back way out of here?" Barnaby nodded with tears in his eyes. "Barnaby, go out the back door," he handed his phone back, "get in your car and drive away. Call the last number dialed and ask them for directions on how to get there. Do you understand me?" Barnaby nodded with muffled whimpers. Loner gave a nod and watched as Barnaby scampered off. As the door closed, there was a metallic click.

"Who's that?" the henchmen screamed.

Loner took a breath. Slipped down his new glasses and peered over top of them. He slowly walked out front.

"That's the guy!" the henchmen screamed.

There were another five henchmen this time. They have slightly heavier weapons this time around. The one from earlier spoke up again, "You in for it now guy! We brought our own super dis time!"

It sounded like the air brakes of a semi-truck. With each step, a metallic foot came in contact with the concrete ground and broken glass as it entered the front of the building. KUR-CLINK. KUR-CLINK. Its torso moved first and was followed by its lower body. It looked like a suit of armor. This thing had a metallic face with a sort of visor. It had a kind of medieval knight feel to the concept of the armor. There was something off about the armor. It's arms. They ended with half a forearm that was rounded. And it's abdomen. What was going on there? It looked as if someone made a tornado in a bottle with water. It was whirling unequally. The machine squared its shoulders. There was a sound that mimicked the sound of cracking thunder. Immediately, whirls emitted from the forearms. They slightly resembled hands.

All of the henchmen hooted and hollered with excitement. Loner continued to peer over the top of the rims of his glasses. "What. In the actual fuck?" he muttered.

Chapter Six: Franchise

Today was a day to show off. Just a little. This would be good. Especially after the broadcasted failure against Loner. The public needed to see a presence. And a new member was just what they needed to see. If his group grew, then the public would support him. Applaud him. Love them. Heroes were what this city needed. The mission today was to make contact with Ripley Greggers. This individual had the gift of manipulating pheromones. Through his research, he had found that Ripley had dabbled and found that he had this ability but couldn't apply it on a grand scale. He was mostly able to use it on groups of insects. Franchise thought to himself, "The next few recruits have to be non-bug related."

He decided to take the helicopter out today. It was a symbol that the people could see. It's something that they would see, and it would give them hope. He turned and saw Fathom peering out the window. Hopper was staring out the other.

He leaned in and tried to yell over the engine, "You wanna try out your new wings?" Hopper had a goofy grin take over his face as he mouthed "Awww yeah."

Franchise leaned in to the cockpit and yelled at Emmitt, "We're going to open the door for a minute." Emmitt gave a chin-up nod. Franchise leaned over to Fathom, "Stay in here, we'll see you at the house." Fathom gave a meek smile.

Franchise leaned over to speak into Hopper's ear. "How bout a race?" Hopper mouthed the words, "you're on." Franchise pulled on the handle and with a whoosh, he somersaulted out. Hopper followed. They were over the city, this was the plan.

Hopper free fell for a minute before tapping the 'H' on his chest. SHHHINK. His wings exploded from his backpack. He slowed in his decent. He was able to lean in either direction to move back and forth. He tapped the 'H' again, and the wings collapsed. He fell a few feet onto a nearby rooftop. Franchise was pretty far ahead. He had had lots of time to play with his equipment and become proficient at it. He zipped over rooftops with speed and grace. Hopper was competitive and wanted to win. He wanted to show Franchise he had a lot to offer. Hopper took off in a sprint. As he came to the end of the rooftop, he flexed and kicked off the edge, propelling himself and leaving gravel in his wake. He cleared the next rooftop altogether. As he touched down, he took off in another sprint. This continued for a couple sets of houses until he had almost caught up with Franchise.

Franchise turned around to witness Hopper gaining on him. A smirk grew on his face. Hopper was a good choice. A good addition. He looked down to the street and saw people watching them in awe. This was what it was all about. This was why the suits. This was why the team. For the people. Franchise decided to show off a bit. He started to swoop in and out from between buildings. He even swooped in to do a lap around Hopper. He chuckled as a surprised look covered hoppers face. They both looked ahead to see the helicopter over their objective. As they continued to approach it, they saw Fathom in the doorway of the helicopter. Normally Emmitt lowered to the ground a little before dropping the ladder. This concerned Franchise a little. Then Fathom fell. As if she fainted. Franchise's heart sunk to the bottom of his feet. Hopper saw it too. They gave each other a frantic look until Franchise pointed his fist in the direction and activated his gyroscope boosters. FFZZZZOOP. He took off. He didn't know if he'll make it. CRRNCH. Hopper propelled off his rooftop. Bound, after bound he continued to meet face to face with Franchise. Each time they met eyes, he spat out a word, "Get. As. Close. As. You. Can." They were running out of rooftops. Franchise whirled as fast as he could. His technology couldn't go any faster. They surpassed all the buildings. Hopper gave one last dig. CRRNCH. He soared past Franchise. As he did, Franchise heard him yell, "Get under me."

Brilliant. He was going to use Franchise as a backstop to drive one last time. Franchise was catching up but not fast enough to catch him before his descent. Franchise yelled, "Hit the H!" Hopper looked back and hit the letter on his chest. SHHINK. Wings exploded from his back, and he drew upwards and backwards. As Franchise situated himself under Hopper, he hit the letter again. SHHHINK. Hopper clambered in the air, then tumbled as he struggled to get his footing on Franchise's shoulders. His equipment wasn't built to sustain more than his weight. They were losing altitude quick. They tumbled further. He dug in his heels and returned them to upright. They sunk further down slowly.

"Off my chest!" Franchise screamed.

Hopper nodded, held on to Franchise with one arm and put both feet on his chest. He looked in the direction of Fathom. Close to the ground. He drove from his legs. In that instant, the two were propelled in different directions. Franchise tumbled feet over head backwards and struck a tree. Hopper soared through the air. His heart stopped. He wasn't going to make it. He watched her descent. She looked peaceful.

Suddenly, she turned to face the ground. She flipped her hands outwards. Small spirals of blue emanated from them. They started to swell around her. As she approached the ground, the swirls completed, forming Miles around her. He mimicked the movements of Fathom inside. Miles' feet hit first. Inside you could see Fathom hit the imaginary ground as she "impacted" and caught herself in a squat. She fell forward and caught herself on the imaginary floor with her right hand. Miles replicated it on the outside on the actual ground. There were slight indents where Miles impacted. As she rose to her feet, Miles followed.

Hopper finally reached the two of them. He started out of breath, "Girl, you scared me half to death!"

Fathom smiled and replied, "Miles wouldn't let me get hurt."

Franchise finally arrived, a little worse for wear. He felt as if he had been hit by a truck. He gasped, "GAH. What happened!"

She replied with another smile, made a fist and threw it in the air while Miles mimicked her, "I won!" You could see Fathom clearly through the open gape of Miles' mouth.

"GAH. UGH. What? That was on purpose!?!"

"Yeah. It was Emmitt's idea," she said.

"You could've DIED!" he screamed, "You don't know how worried we were. We thought you were in trouble!"

She gave a slight pout from being scolded and offered, "I did a superhero landing."

Franchise stood speechless. Trying to catch his breath. Hopper turned and replied, "Yeah, I was here. It was pretty sweet."

The pout left her face as she said, "Yeah I was like WA-POWP." As she said the words, she (and Miles) jumped and mimicked the landing and punching of the ground.

Franchise tried to remain stern, but his stiff upper lip slowly left his face. He returned, "That was pretty cool." He furrowed his eyebrows, "Why were you IN Miles?"

Fathom (and Miles) shrugged. "I don't know. I asked him to catch me. When he came out, he was around me."

Franchise fell into the back of his mind. Fascinating. A kind of symbiotic relationship with her imaginary friend. Extraordinary.

He continued, "Well, put him away for now. And Hopper…" Hopper looked up. "Don't kick me again."

Hopper chuckled and said, "You gotta admit, that was kinda cool too."

Everyone gave a few chuckles. The helicopter flew overhead as Emmitt took off. A few new trucks turned onto the street.

Hopper had a confused look on his face, "Why the news always shows up and never the cops?"

Fathom looked at Franchise and he replied, "That is funny, huh?"

He knew the answer, he just didn't want to explain it to the other two. He had made a few more donations. He explained with his donations to both the police and the news that the news would follow him after his donation. And if the news captured something that the cops needed to intervene, then they would come and intervene. There were a lot of donations made. The short version was Franchise promised not to harm anyone and let the cops do their jobs. If they let him do his superhero theatrical thing, then he'd donate a very healthy sum, annually. And news always needed news. They received "donations" to follow some of the most heroic news around. They would probably stay back farther this time since the last "recruitment" ended so violently.

The three of them arrived at the prospective house. Franchise knocked on the door and rang the doorbell twice. There was no answer. He knocked again and rang the bell. There was a flurry at the curtains as someone peered through. Franchise was a little concerned. Why don't they answer the door?

"Hello?" He called into the door.

"GO AWAY," the door boomed.

"I'm sorry to disturb you, but my name is Franchise. I am here to talk to Ripley Greggers. Is he here?"

The door cracked open, and a woman's face entered into view. "What do you know about my Ripley? Have they found him?"

Franchise asked with concern, "Found him?"

She opened the door a little more and then looked up and down at the costumed figures. "Where are you guys from?" she asked.

"Ma'am," Franchise started, "we are the Heroes for the People. Young Ripley is special. He has a gift that he can use to help his city."

She looked concerned, "His science…bug…stuff?"

Franchise smiled and returned, "Yes ma'am, his science bug stuff." His face grew concerned as well, and he asked, "Could we come in? You asked if we found him. I'd like to know more about that and see if we can help."

She gave a resistant nod and allowed them in. They walked into the house, and the first thing he noticed were newspapers everywhere. The woman started, "He disappeared two weeks ago. No one knows where he went, and the police can't find him. We haven't had news in days."

She was distressed. Franchise continued to scan the environment and asked, "How old is Ripley now?"

"Thirteen," she responded.

"And you are his…?"

"Mother," she responded.

They sit down and talk for twenty or so minutes. There really wasn't much to learn or talk about. Ripley went out for groceries and didn't come back. No one had news or development. Franchise promised he would keep an eye out and let her know if they found any information on him. She thanked them and showed a bit of relief.

They were getting ready to leave, and Franchise asked, "Can I see his room real quick, see if it gives us any leads?"

Ripley's mother shrugged and said, "The cops already did. It hasn't been touched since then. It's down the hall on the left." Franchise nodded and told the others to hang tight and that he'll only be a second.

He headed down the hallway. He entered the room, took a breath, and began to focus. Analyzing. The room fell black. There was nothing, not even a trace. Suddenly, he felt a tug on his pants, looked down to see a small black cat with white feet and tips on its ears.

"Come here Mittens," Franchise heard a call from behind him.

He turned to lock eyes with a small eight-year-old girl. Her eyes gave off a blueish glow. A grin grew on his face as he faded back from analyzing.

"Hello there. And what is your name young hero?"

She responded with a frail, "Gracie."

Franchise took a knee and started petting the cat so he could look up to Gracie. He began, "Gracie Greggers, huh?" She nodded. "I'm here for your brother, but he's not here."

She nodded again. He offered out his hand and said, "I am Franchise. I am a Hero for the People." He leaned in and asked in a low voice, "Did you know about your brother's….gift?"

She gave him a blank stare. He continued, "It's OK, I'm one of the good guys. I was here to see if he wanted to help me take care of the city."

She smiled. Franchise looked her in the eyes and in a whisper asked, "You have a gift too, huh?" She looked over her shoulder, apparently looking for her mother. She turned back and gave a small smile and nod. "And what can you do young hero?"

She leaned in and whispered, "I can talk to animals."

Franchise's face lit up. "Can you now? Can I saw? Can you show me?"

She furrowed her brow a bit, "Other people can't hear them, just me."

He shrugged his shoulders and responded convincingly, "That's OK, could you still show me?

She felt reassured. She knelt next to Mittens. She put her hand under the cat's chin and lifted its face to meet hers, and she furrowed her brow again. The two slipped into a distant gaze.

Analyzing. The room became black again. But the sight was astounding. From Gracie's eye's there was a helix of energy emitting into the cats. It moved in one direction only. Amazing. This was no communication at all. This was mind control! Simple at best. But as she developed and learned, she would be able to grow her ability as well.

He faded back into reality. And said lowly, "Gracie?" She snapped out of her trance. He continued, "That was wonderful." She gave a meek smile. He started again, "If you continue to talk to Mittens every day, soon other people would be able to hear her too. Keep up the good work."

Gracie felt accomplished with Franchise's praise. He leaned in again, "And Gracie?" She looked him in the eye. "Does your mother know about this?"

She shook her head no and responded, "She thought I just made it up."

Franchise responded, "Good. Don't let anyone know about this. Keep practicing, and I will be back. Once you are older, you can help me keep the city safe."

She gave another small smile and a nod for confirmation. Franchise stood up and walked to the front of the house and thanked Ms. Greggers. "Thank you for your time Ma'am. If we find anything, we'll be sure to let you know." She shook his hand with a smile.

The three heroes exited the house, and Hopper asked, "What's next? Back to HQ?"

"No Hopper. There is still work to be done," Franchise replied. "This wasn't a bust in the slightest."

After meeting Gracie, he thought gifts might be hereditary. "Do you have a brother or sister Hopper?" Hopper shook his head no. He turned to Fathom and then continued walking. "We still have half a day left. We can go talk to Madalyn McCray. We're only about a twenty-minute walk away."

"So, this Ripley guy, he can attract bugs?" asked Hopper.

"He can manipulate pheromones. He can attract or discourage different species. Some species entire lives are manipulated by pheromones, like bees," Franchise explained.

"So, he was going help us gather bees?" Hopper asked confused.

"That is only his capacities now. With time and practice, I believe he could affect any species," Franchise said proudly of his knowledge.

"So, what's the deal with this girl we're going to see now?" Hopper pressed.

"She has an ability for comprehension." He was met with blank stares from his two partners. He continued, "She can understand, comprehend, and speak any language instantly."

Fathom looked impressed, "That's cool."

"I agree," Franchise chimed, equally impressed.

They each think the trip was better on foot than whizzing through the city again. Even though the reporters were creeping behind them in their camera crew vehicles. They turned onto the street where Madalyn worked, and the common people gave the costumed members odd and strange looks. Madalyn worked at a bookstore on this street. The three heroes continued down the street, giving greetings of the day only to not have them returned. This was not the reception Franchise had envisioned at all. They found her bookstore and walked in. Once again, they did not receive a warm welcome.

Franchise walked to the front counter and asked, "Hello there, my name is Franchise. Is there a Madalyn McCray that works here?"

His request was met with a glance of judgement. "Hello?" a meek voice called from behind a bookcase. The heroes walked around to come face to face with a woman in her late thirties sitting in a wheelchair.

"Madalyn?" Franchise asked.

"Uh yes?" she responded. She was taken aback by all the strangely dressed people.

Franchise knelt down and got eye level with her. "Ms. McCray. I am Franchise, and we are the Heroes for the People." Madalyn looked concerned and not receptive. "You have a gift, Madalyn. And I want you to help us keep the city safe with it."

Madalyn does not look amused as she said, "Who put you up to this?"

Franchise's face grew concerned, "What do you mean?"

She took a deep breath and shot back, "You might as well just spit in my face. You come into my place of work, dressed like that?

You come to an old disabled woman in a wheelchair, and you ask for my help? To help this city? Get out."

Franchise's look of concern turned into a look of pity. "Madalyn, you don't know how special you really were. You have an amazing gift."

She spat back, "So I can speak another language, so can half of this country."

Franchise leaned in and spoke softly, "But none of them can speak ALL languages." She raised an eyebrow. "Please, humor me at least. Please. At least take a walk with us."

His two teammates cringed as Madalyn scowled. Franchise closed his eyes as he realized his mistake. And then he started again, "Ten minutes of your time?" She inhaled through her nose and let out her breath through her mouth. And finally spoke, "ten minutes." They pushed her to a local park.

"How exactly can I help you and your merry band of misfits?" she pried.

Hopper pushed Madalyn, so Franchise could look her in the face while they talk.

"Communication is the most important piece of helping someone or getting them to understand. So much is lost through poor interpretation. And you have the ability to negate that. You can ensure that everyone in the world has a chance to comprehend in their native tongue."

She responded, "So, I'm an interpreter?"

Franchise looked her in the eyes and smiled, "The best there is."

She fought back a smile. Franchise stooped and looked her in the eyes, "You do have limitations. But with language, you do not. You have a gift, a wonderful one. Would you help us by helping this city?"

She broke eye contact and looked in the distance. She covered her mouth and started to wipe tears from her eyes, "It's been a long time since I had a purpose."

Franchise smiled bigger and stated, "You're going to need a name."

Hopper backed up from the chair and put his hands in the air. "Hold on now. Hey lady you better pick your own before these two pick a wacky one like fricken Hopper." He said as he pointed two thumbs back at himself. Everyone laughed.

Fathom squealed, "OOOHH, what is it called when, a bunch of words, that uh…only certain groups of people use?"

Madalyn laughed through her tears. She gave her cheeks another wipe. "Lingo, dear, it's called Lingo."

"Oooooh, I like it. It's fancy," Fathom applauded.

Hopper looked directly at Franchise, "Dang mayne! She got to name TWO people?" Everyone laughed again.

"Lingo it is then," Franchise started, "we'll give you a couple of days to prepare. I'll make accommodations at HQ. For now, let's get you back to your work." Lingo agreed.

As they finished their walk through the park, they headed back to her work. As they turned onto her street, the group saw two individuals standing on the sidewalk near the entrance to the bookstore. They looked very out of place. The man was tall, old, and skinny. He had on skintight black pants and a sleeveless black vest. The vest was opened to the front with no undershirt which showed off his birdcage chest. He had long stringy black and grey hair that billowed around the dingy top hat he wore. His bony fingers gripped a cigarette, that he drew into his pursed, thin, and cracked lips. The other was a female. She was stocky and stout. She wore a long burgundy and gold crusted dress. She had a pair of gold steam punk goggles perched on top of her head.

"Oy there mate," the slimy thin man spat in a thick Australian accent. As he spoke, smoke billowed from his crooked and terribly yellowed teeth.

"Could we help you with something?" Franchise asked plainly.

The man pointed one of his bony fingers at Lingo and took another drag off his cigarette. It billowed out of his nose. "She's commin wit us," he grumbled.

The team squared up, and Hopper announced, "Them's some pretty big words. You a bit outnumbered, weren't you?"

The man drew deeply on his cigarette and let it out. "You hear'em der Mirrors?" he said over his shoulder while lighting another cigarette with the butt of the first.

"I hear 'em," Mirrors said as she pulled down her goggles. She cracked her neck left. Then right. In front of her, to her left, with a blink appeared an identical person. That looked just like her. With another blink, one appeared to her right. All three in unison spoke, "That even it up, huh, Smoke?"

Smoke took another long drag off his cigarette until the cherry hit the filter. "Last chance," he bellowed as he flicked his butt at the group. No one moved. Smoke finished filling his lungs with a deep breath in. He then hunched over as thick black smoke flooded the streets and rose into the air.

Franchise couldn't see anything. He screamed, "Fathom! You and Miles get Lingo outta here! Hopper get in the air and get eyes on these guys!" He turned and lost himself in the back of his head.

Analyzing. Particles of the smoke around him lit up with a dim glow. Smoke had the ability to manipulate and replicate particles of the air on a massive scale. He faded out of his trance as he began to gag and cough. It was the smoke from the cigarette. Smoke had replicated it. Franchise couldn't breathe. His lungs burned. CRRNCH. He heard Hopper take off. He aimed his wrist in the air. When he tried to flick it to engage his thrusters, he got hit from the side.

"GAH," he screamed.

The sucker punch made him gasp for air. He was thrown into a coughing fit. He needed to get into the air. He looked up. Nothing but black smoke. He stood and out of the corner of his eye he saw pale skin and then, CRACK. He was hit with another sucker punch.

"Samatter der greenie?" Smoke scoffed, "Ya haffin a bita troubles are ye?"

CRACK. Another punch. Franchise was gasping for air. Smoke kept coming back. Franchise had to break contact and go up for air. He touched his left forearm. SHHHINK. His crossbow engaged. He pressed the tip of the bolts. His lungs burned. They thirsted for air. He thrusted his fist in the air. As soon as he went to flick his wrists, he turned completely around and forced an uppercut. FZZZZT.

"YEEEARRGGGG!" Smoke screamed as the tips of the bolts made contact

Franchise thrusted his fist back into the air and flicked his wrist instantly. FZZZZTHHOOOP. His gyroscopes engaged as he thrusted into the air. Past the smoke cloud. Air! He gasped and coughed. In the air, he searched around frantically.

The smoke started to dissipate. "Hopper!" he screamed.

Hopper returned, "We gotta problem Moneyman…"

Franchise turned to see Hopper sifting through the air with his wings. "Talk to me!" Franchise barked.

Hopper pointed, "Fathom is over there with Lingo inside of Miles. That Mirrors chick trying to get at 'em."

"What are we waiting for?" barked Franchise.

Hopper pointed with both his hands in different directions. "That Mirrors chick is also pushing Lingo in THAT direction and THAT direction."

Sure enough, there was the burgundy dress, and gold goggle donned Mirrors pushing Lingo up 5th, and down 13th. He drew in another breath.

Analyzing.... Each of the three Mirrors lit up like a Christmas tree. Projections maybe? He faded back.

"You go after that one; I'll go after that one," Franchise instructed.

Hopper nodded and hit the letter on his chest and dropped. Franchise tilted in the direction of his target and blasted off. He got within throwing distance. He grabbed at his belt, reared back and screamed, "Benjamin's Bolas!"

WHIIRRRL. CRACK. It spun through the air and popped open and glided towards Mirrors. It made contact. And with a blink, they were gone. He gave a quick breath and muttered, "Projections."

He took off in Fathom's direction. When he arrived, Hopper came from the other direction. "She just disappeared!" he cried out.

"I know Hopper," Franchise reassured. "Fathom? How you holding up?" he yelled as they approached her.

She was gritting her teeth as she strained. This was too much for her. Franchise grabbed at his belt again and reared back. He let go a second time yelling, "Benjamin's bolas!"

WHIIIIIRRRL. CRACK. It spun and split open again. Once it connected, Mirrors flickered with the impact, then her and Lingo vanished. The three looked at each other.

Fathom started, "Where'd Lingo go? She was just here."

Franchise gritted his teeth, "A fourth projection."

He flipped around and zipped over to where he had fought Smoke. Nothing. Gone. He hovered in the air. News crews flooded the immediate areas. They had lost. They couldn't save one of their own. He failed. He looked over at the other two. They looked at him for guidance and answers. He shook his head. He had none.

Chapter Seven: Loner

Another metallic foot pressed its weight into the fallen glass on the ground. Loner gazed into the room full of angry thugs. And a suit of armor. With little tornadoes for hands. His days had gotten stranger and stranger. Loner slinked into a fighting stance and propped up his hands.

"You ain't got no chance this time Punch-y! We ready for you dis time," the thug that ran away the first time recited, so everyone could hear.

Loner was paying attention to the thugs in the room. He would make short work of them. Especially now that he could see. He was more concerned about Tornado hands. He caught a glimpse of something etched into the chest plate of the metallic figure. Loner's eyes widened. He saw a familiar letter S and C in triangles. These nut sacks worked for SYNERGY. If the monsters he was chasing down were from Dr. Monroe, was this a product of the Engineer? And did that mean the gangs that were controlling small businesses; were also working for SYNERGY? This was getting too big and Loner was in the middle of it. Twice.

Loner didn't want to get caught up in this. He still had to complete the job for Dr. Monroe. He didn't want to get tied to any of this and get dragged deeper into this mess. But there was no good way out. The henchmen were getting restless as they stood in silence looking at each other.

One of the thugs broke the silence. "Uh, you wan' us to uh, shoot him?"

The coward in charge agreed. On his command, Loner set into a flex. He felt his muscles tighten and he was able to look through his glasses normally. He was able to see. It was amazing. He looked down as he saw bullets strike his chest and arms. They crumpled as they hit and ricocheted away. He pivoted and drove off his back foot. He launched himself at one of the cronies. He cocked back a fist, and once he was nearly chest to chest, he unwound his punch downward into the crook of his neck and shoulder. The poor thug folded in half and then fell forward. Half of the gunmen stopped firing as they fell into shock and awe. Loner didn't care if he smeared these wastes of life. He realized what all the pieces together meant. He had been working for the wrong team. He had been acquiring weapons for the same people bullying the innocent for profit and status. This was what they deserved. Loner was fine with wiping this filth from existence. If they were willing to take a life, then so was he. He stood there absorbing a few more rounds and then picked up the crumpled thug in front of him and hurled him into another. They crunched against the wall. He sprinted towards two in the corner and grabbed one by the neck. He closed his fist tightly as a gurgle and pop resounded throughout the front of the building. He jumped, still with the thug in hand, and threw an overhand haymaker into the next thug. The Terror-cane stood silent and did not interact. Just the constant hum and whirl of its hands. The coward thug had finished his clip and gave a quick look around to see if they still had the upper hand. Once he realized he didn't, he attempted to run again.

GRRT. Loner unflexed. He also glanced at his work. He walked over to the crushed thug imbedded into the wall. On the way, he picked up shards of broken glass. He grabbed the head of the sputtering thug in the wall, flexed, and jerked his neck. CRICKT. He walked outside and saw the coward peeling off down the street. He drove off his feet and covered the distance in no time. Loner threw the broken glass, impaling the thug through the back. He fell onto his face. Loner walked up and stepped on the back of his neck with a CRICKT. He didn't need to go grab help again. He walked back to the building. The cops would probably show soon. He approached the metal man. It still hadn't moved. Maybe it malfunctioned.

Loner looked closely, and then said aloud, "You could take the fall then."

When Loner went to leave, Terror-cane turned to face him. As Loner drew back a punch, a cone of wind erupted from the right arm. It hit Loner like a ton of bricks and propelled him backward. As he felt the initial punch of impact, he instinctively flexed. He spun in circles with the vortex and teared through the wall behind him. Eventually, he was flung off one side of the vortex as it continued to tear down the street. Loner struck the ground and rolled a few feet. He tried to catch his breath and stand. He peered up as Terror-cane walked outside into the rubble. One discharge from his arm tore a truck-sized hole through the building. Loner had to tear this machine apart before it teared into the apartments nearby. He unflexed, took a breath, then sprinted in its direction. Terror-cane aimed the opposite arm and discharged another torrent of wind. Loner flexed as he headed straight into it. It was like nothing he had ever felt. The force was astounding. He felt like he was being crushed from all sides. He leaned into it and dug his feet into the asphalt. The force of the torrent continued to drive him back as he left gouge marks in the pavement. Loner continued to lose ground, and he fell into a three, and then a four point stance trying to withstand the sheer force. He left claw marks and gouges down the street. Terror-cane lifted its other arm as it erupted another vortex. As it connected with Loner, he spun out of control and tumbled through a street sign into a vehicle which crumpled around him.

The Engineer:

The Engineer sat behind his console. The pictures through Terror-canes' point of vision were displayed on the screen. He leaned to speak over his shoulder, "Does this demonstration suffice?"

Boss Winston replied, "It is impressive that you are able to control the super's ability within that suit of yours. But I asked you to show me what it was capable of."

Dr. Monroe chimed in, "Congratulations Engineer. You created a leaf blower."

The Engineer pursed his lips then sucked his teeth. He turned to the screen and cracked his neck. He stood for a second, then walked to one of his shelves where he retrieved a multi piece contraption. He sat back at his console and started attaching it to his temples and parts of his head. On the screen, Loner was able to get back to his feet and started to make his way back to Terror-cane. The Engineer continued to assemble his machination. Loner drove off his feet in a flex; then upper cutted the metal man. It was driven into the air by the sheer force. It reflected in the visual picture on the Engineer's computer. It made contact with the ground. The Engineer continued to click pieces in place.

Boss Winston started, "Whatever you are doing Engineer, we are about to lose my weapon because of it."

The Engineer had assembled the device that connected to his temples, the front of his forehead and the base of his skull. He plugged it into a control panel the size of a laptop. He started typing and plugging in different components to it.

Dr. Monroe continued to belittle him, "He is finally consumed by his inferior capability and is trying to download hooked on phonics from the internet." On the screen, Terror-cane had hit the ground and stayed there. The picture of Loner was displayed as he grew nearer. The Engineer hit a button on his console, and a drawer slid out. He reached in and pulled out two gauntlet looking devices. He plugged the console into the gloves, and the gloves into the box connected to his headset. He replied simply, "Simple commands yield simple results. I can now communicate better."

Loner approached the grounded wind machine. As he grew nearer, it pushed itself up to one knee. Loner drove off his back foot into the air. He flexed and reared back a punch. Terror-cane shifted its weight and placed its arm under Loner and launched a wind spout, launching Loner backwards through the air. The Engineer manipulated its arms downward and created a whirlwind around its lower body propelling upward. The Engineer continued to manipulate it, following Loner's path through the air. Loner was in his descent. He was falling. Helpless. Terror-cane maneuvered over top of Loner, and the whirlwind stopped. Both the arms were pressed together, and a vortex erupted from them. Loner flexed in an effort to reduce the collateral damage. In an instant, he was corkscrewed into the ground. Terror-cane resumed his whirlwind and returned to the ground. He walked to the impact site of Loner. When Terror-cane looked within the crater, he saw nothing. Loner erupted out of the asphalt behind him. Upon hearing the impact of the erupting ground, the torso of Terror-cane rotated in place. Both of his arms collided and set off a vortex, slugging Loner. He tumbled out of control. Loner unflexed. This guy could move. His head screamed, and his sides ached. This Terror-cane was fast. And when he connected, it was like getting hit with cinderblocks. The only way he was going to gain any headway was a melee fight. But he was wearing down, quick. He charged. Terror-cane whipped up another wave. Loner flexed and kicked off to the side. As soon as he connected with dirt, he pushed off and attempted to complete a couple of boxing combinations. They were met with calculated responses from the Engineer. Counter punched backed by cyclonic force followed dips and ducks. It was an elegant dance. The Engineer being the lead.

Doctor Monroe seemed to compliment, "Didn't foresee boxing being your strong suit."

The Engineer responded, "Simple mathematical application. Simpleton."

Every third or fourth punch Loner was losing ground and position. He continued to fail to connect. He tried to break contact through leaping away. He was met with the whirlwind of Terror-cane. With another gust, he was pinned to the ground. As Loner tried to rise to his feet, he felt a mechanical knee in his chest. The stump of its mechanical arm was thrust against his face and then activated. His head was whipped back and forth as he held onto his flex. It was met with the other arm as the vortex intensified. Loner grabbed both of its arms and tried to advance his current position. It was impossible. He felt himself losing the flex. He started to fade. Black started to creep into the edges of his sight. He felt rubble shoot up from the sides of his face as the vortexes drilled into the ground past him. His body couldn't hold on against the sheer force. The blackness took over. His arms fell helplessly to his sides.

Loner:

Loner pried his eyes open. Everything was blurry. He tried to comprehend his surroundings. He attempted to roll over. Sharp pains in his head and neck. He reached his hand to his face and felt shards of his glasses embedded. He pulled large shards out. He rolled to his side and tried to gather what was going on around him. The street was littered with flashing lights. The cops did show up. Cop cars were getting launched through the air at the whim of powerful whirlwinds. Gun fire. Screams of unprepared policemen. They were no match. Chunks of a nearby building were being ripped apart. Terror-cane continued to decimate the street and police force. Loner tried to open his jaw, and his neck clicked. He grumbled in agony. He started to drag himself out of the street using his arms. Cars continued to tumble end over end, through the air as the police continued to lose their struggle. Loner started to drag his knees up to help him propel faster. He was of no use to the poor police officers. At least they were a prominent distraction to allow him to get to safety. As he continued to shamble into an alleyway, he felt fizzles and sparks on his neck. He fought through the ache and pain as he reached behind his neck. He slowly was able to grasp at a small button-shaped device with an antenna. He grunted through moving his arm back. Loner flicked it back into the street. It was hard for him to comprehend. But that's probably how they found him after the loud mouth ran back to tell them a super with super strength interfered. He continued to inch down the dark alleyway. He needed somewhere to hide. He was in no condition to help. He could barely keep inching away from Terror-cane. He hit resistance. He lifted his head slowly. He had run into the bottom of a fire escape. Loner reached out with his right arm, grabbed hold and pulled himself onto it. He groaned in agony and continued this arduous process for three flights until he collapsed in the corner. He coughed and sputtered. Eventually, he closed his eyes. Outside grew silent. He breathed in. He breathed out.

His eyes opened slowly. He lifted his head. He was inside. He tried to sit up and was reminded thoroughly of the beating he had received. He felt as if he had broken glass under his skin. He reached down and realized he was only wearing his blue jeans. Someone had wrapped his ribs with gauze and tape. He slowly lowered his head and laid it on its side. It looked to be someone's living room. The furniture was in rough shape. Old and dingy. Next to the window, there was broken glass and debris under it. The window didn't seem damaged. The people who live here must've dragged him in through their window from the fire escape. He was bandaged thoroughly. Even his bag made it in. It was open, and his books were next to it with two sets of glasses. He didn't mind. Curiosity happened when you dragged a half dead person through your window. He continued to scan the room until he locked eyes with a small boy sitting in the doorway. He had a dark complexion with a small painted red dot on his forehead. Loner gave a frail smile.

The boy tilted his head and shouted over his shoulder, "Ma Ma, Pa Pa, he's awake."

His parents entered the room with concerned faces. The father had a cup of water in his hands. The mother stayed back in the doorway. The man spoke, but Loner couldn't understand him.

The boy spoke up, "water."

The man offered his hand out to help Loner sit up. It was a slow process, but eventually, Loner was upright and accepted the cup with another small smile. He glanced up. The parents had similar features as the son including the same painted dot on the foreheads.

Loner offered, "Thank you," while looking the family in the eyes.

"They don't know what to think of you," the boy stated plainly. He continued, "We saw you save the eye doctor. They liked that. They didn't let me watch when you fought the other men. They didn't like that. They saw you try to stop the metal robot. They didn't know if you were good or bad. I told them you were good."

Loner smirked and offered, "Well then thank you. What's your name kid?"

"Kevin. Kevin Bambang. These are my mom and dad, Annisa and Fadhlan Bambang. They don't speak English very well," Kevin said.

Loner responded with another smirk, "I see that."

Kevin went on, "They were going to leave you on the fire escape. I didn't let them. I had to remind them it wasn't in good faith."

Loner chuckled. As he laughed, twinges run up and down his bones. It felt as if there was sand under his skin, and if he moved sandpaper was being run across it. He winced and shuttered. While sulking and being absorbed by his injuries, he asked, "Kevin? Could you thank them for me?"

Kevin spoke a few words in another language. "Kevin?" Loner started again, "Who bandaged me?"

"Oh, that's my dad. He's a vet," Kevin said plainly. "Why don't you have a costume?"

Loner doesn't like attention. This kid was fine, but he doesn't want to let him down. It was because of this kid that he was upright today. Loner offered, "I don't know. I guess I never found the time."

Kevin shot back, "Every hero needs a costume." Loner smiled back.

Loner stayed for a few days. He spent most of his time playing with Kevin and watching the parents perform foreign rituals from their culture. They even tried to involve him in a few. One of which he knelt next to a cabinet. The cabinet was open, and a candle was lit, and Fadhlan would ring a bell and sit and remain silent. Loner would kneel with him. After some time, Fadhlan would open his eyes and offer Loner a smile and shake his hand. During Loner's downtime without the scrutiny of the family, he relentlessly searched his clothes for other tracking devices. This family saved him. They did not deserve a visit from SYNERGY for their kindness. Each attempt produced no results. Thankfully. Late nights consisted of Kevin asking about the adventures of Loner. Loner told him about the circus and being raised by a strongman. He told him of some of the things he came across in his adventures. He kept it mostly "G" rated. He talked about his encounter with Franchise.

Kevin asked, "Why don't you join them? They seem like they want to help. And you helped the eye doctor."

"I might," Loner told the child. Once again, he didn't want to disappoint the poor kid. Kevin perked up and ran out of the room. He returned shortly with Loner's hoodie. He handed it over. The tears and holes from Terror-cane and previous encounters were patched. As he turned it over to the front, there was a large dark blue felt letter "L" sewn onto the chest. Loner looked up at Kevin and cocked an eyebrow. Kevin whispered, "Every hero needs a costume." Loner chuckled and put it on.

"I'm leaving tomorrow, Kevin," Loner said. A sad and concerned look grew on Kevin's face. "Thank you for everything."

"Heroes take care of people," Kevin said reassuring himself.

"Yes, they do," Loner responded as he looked down at his slipshod felt 'L'. He was pretty sure the kid had cut it and sewed it on. He didn't have the heart to tell the kid he hates it. He petted it. Looked up. And gave Kevin a reassuring nod.

He left early the next morning, so as not to make a big scene with the family. He found the nearest ATM and attempted using his SYNERGY card. He inserted it, and instantly money came out of the machine. He thumbed through it. Five hundred dollars. He slinked back up to the fire escape of their apartment, slid up the window, and placed it in the cabinet where he had sat with Fadhlan.

It had been days since the conflict with Terror-cane. He stopped by a convenience store and swiped his SYNERGY card for two packs of cigarettes and a lighter. He struck up his cigarette and took a look around. He oriented himself and started walking in the direction of his hotel. Hopefully they held his room. After an hour of walking, he arrived at the hotel. He walked in the front door and took off towards his room. There was still a 'do not disturb' sign on the door. Odd. If SYNERGY knew where he was, and sent someone after him, why didn't they send someone to his room? He opened the door. Nothing was touched. Odd. Inside his bag was the SYNERGY phone. He still had a job to do. He really didn't feel up to it. He really didn't feel up to boxing a wind robot man either. He picked up the phone. He looked at it hard. He slumped into a chair and rustled through his bag. He cracked open his notebook and scribbled new findings. He drew a rough sketch of Terror-cane into it and what he found it could do. He opened the file on Gorge and thumbed through it. He reached down to his ribs and gave them a squeeze. Still tender. He let out a long, exaggerated sigh. He picked up the phone again. Looked at it hard. And dialed the number.

The phone picked up, and Doctor Monroe's voice was on the other end, "Yes?"

"Hey, what're your last coordinates on my target?" Loner responded.

"Same as when you were briefed. But it's been a few days. He may have moved. Were there complications?" Dr. Monroe pried.

"Naw, not really, just got spun around," Loner replied. "I'm on it; I'll give you a call in the next day or so." CLICK. Dr. Monroe hung up the phone and turned around. He approached the intercom on his wall. He pressed and held the button. BZZT. "Mr. Winston. The Loner is still alive."

Loner dropped the phone and sparked up another cigarette. It had been a long time since he'd been overpowered by something. The sheer force of the wind of Terror-cane was incredible. There was little he could do. What if he was walking into a similar situation with Gorge. He still wasn't a hundred percent. He probably wouldn't be for quite some time. He took a drag off his cigarette and said, "Welp, let's go get this cow guy." He gathered his things and checked out of the hotel. He contemplated going to see Barnaby. He felt it best to leave him be. He set out to the slaughterhouse depicted in the information received from Dr. Monroe. It took Loner about a day to get there. The trip itself was uneventful. When he arrived was a different story altogether.

When he approached the slaughterhouse, it was something that one would expect to find in gothic horror stories. The building was dilapidated and run down. As he walked into the compound, he smelled the odor of stale blood. For a second he had flashbacks of his encounter with Meat. He walked through the doors to the building and looked around. There were pieces and parts from an assortment of animals. There were barely scraps remaining. He scoured the entire farm from top to bottom. The creature seemed to have broken into the cow area first. After it worked through the entire barn, it moved through chicken, ducks, goats, and ended by wiping out the entire pig population on this farm.

Whatever this thing started as, it had worked through the entire farm. Loner walked through the entire slaughterhouse first, and then through the entire farm. There was not a trace of a single living thing left on the entire grounds of the slaughterhouse. There were smears of where animals and people used to be. Loner followed the trail through a small town. It was also wiped out. He grew concerned. If this thing consumed an entire farm of cows, then it would resemble some sort of bovine horror. But it had started to devour humans. What was he going to encounter next? Loner continued to follow his trail of gore and mangled remains until he stood in front of a tall building. Loner was in disbelief. He shook his head from side to side. He read the sign "Sacred Grace Memorial Hospital."

"What. In the actual fuck," he said to himself.

The parking lot leading up to the hospital was dismantled. Cars and barriers littered throughout. The tops and sides of the vehicles were torn backwards like pop top aluminum cans. Not much remained. There were massive tracks leading into the facility. There were two different sets. The back feet were massive separated hoofs, two in front and one smaller one in the rear. They must be at least two feet long, by one foot wide each. The front prints were a mash-up of giant, one foot by one foot, human-like palms with hoof imprints where fingers would be. Loner stared at these prints, and then behind him. What had he walk into? Why hadn't these people called for help? They probably had. But SYNERGY probably had their fingers in it. He grabbed at his ribs.

They were still tender. He didn't know if he was ready for this. His meet up with Meat went well because Meat didn't really fight back. And Terror-cane almost killed him. Loner had no way to counteract that. So, what about this? He wasn't healed from his last encounter.

He looked up at the front entrance. The doors were ripped down into the building. There were the hoofed talon markings gashed through the wall. The light flickered on and off. Loner looked up. Blood spatters and more hoofed talon marks. Loner proceeded with caution. He slowly investigated the first floor, room by room, and then section by section. He became even more disturbed and uneasy as he continued. Each room, each operatory, each admin cubical: wiped clean. It didn't look like anyone escaped. Just smudges, of where people used to be. Loner grew solemn and started to realize the severity of this reality. He may not make it out of here. He passed by elevator doors. They had come off the hinges and sputtered sparks as the lights fought to stay lit. Stairs it was. He pushed on. More scratches and scrapes. More smudges and stains. No bones. No pieces. Just smudges and stains.

He climbed the stairs to the second floor. Two out of six. The stairs had claw marks and crushed rubble around where this thing had walked. He stepped out and made sure the door didn't slam behind him. It was dark. Lights flickered on and off. He slinked cautiously down the hallway. He started to work on the math. Gorge doubled in size after consuming his body weight. If he started out human at a hundred and eighty pounds, he'd put on a lot of weight by now. If he was big before the cows, he'd double in size by the first cow. Each cow was roughly twenty-four hundred pounds. Just with the thirty cows alone at the slaughterhouse, he would have grown five times. And after eating the rest of the slaughterhouse and pigs, that'd make six times. That would take a lot of people to work on number seven. Even by his sloppy math, this thing was probably around 40,000 pounds. Half the size of a semi-truck. Pushing the limit of the second floor of this six-story building. It couldn't climb any higher. If it got bigger, it would fall through. Loner stopped. There was nowhere to go. He looked down the hallway. The ceiling and one wall of the hallway were gouged out. He stopped and listened. There was a sloppy slapping sound accompanied with pops and crunching noises. Loner froze. He'd been stupid enough to climb to the second story and come face to face with a semi-truck sized monster; which ate: a slaughterhouse, a town, and a hospital full of people. And there was nowhere to go. How? Why? This was idiotic. Why did SYNERGY send HIM though? Especially if he was defeated by Terror-cane? He heard a gruff and a snort. Then the snapping of jaws. And then scraping and shifting. It was turning around. It was too big for this 'tiny' environment. This was it. He dropped his satchel near the doorway. If there was an upper hand, it'll have to be now. He took a deep breath in and jutted down the hallway. His pace lessened when his eyes met the hole the monster pushed in to access the room. He halted and froze. It had turned around. And Loner was now face to face with the monstrosity.

The beast filled the entire room. There were only a few sheer feet of clearance around it. Its eyes had been pushed to the outside of its face, like the position of a cow or boar. A third of its body was made of its massive head which came out to a prominent snout. It had small bull horns that seemed dwarfed next to large ears on either side of its head. In between its ears ran a Mohawk, like a wild boar, that ran down to its haunches. The monsters' rear legs seem incapacitated by the beast's own weight. They seemed lame and only there to stabilize the monstrosity. The grotesque monster dug its front hoof-clawed hands into the floor. Its upper jaw, in line with its shoulders, drew open. Heavy heated breathes resonated out. Its open mouth was riddled with an assortment of giant jagged and dull teeth. Its open gape matches the size of the door it crushed through.

"GRRRREEEEOOOOAAAARRRRR," bellowed from its open mouth.

"Fuck. Me. Running," Loner said quietly.

Chapter Eight: Franchise

The smoke was still dissipating throughout the sky. Franchise looked around frantically. He phased in and out, trying to tap into his ability. Trying to track down Lingo. Trying to find Smoke. Trying to find Mirrors. Trying to find anyone.

"I still don't see 'em," echoed Hopper.

"Keep looking!" Franchise screamed.

This couldn't happen. The others couldn't see this. Not failure. Everything was unraveling. He had to find her. The good guys had to win. We had to win. We couldn't lose one of our own. They had to be somewhere close. He frantically searched, zipping from one location to the next. Hopper came into view from time to time as he propelled into sight, suspended in the air, and then descended.

Franchise's mind raced. His eyes flew rapidly in all directions. Looking for a hint, a scrap, a clue, just something. He applied his power on and off without any success. He looked down at the ground to lock eyes with a concerned Fathom and Hopper. Hopper cupped his mouth with his hands, "What now?"

Franchise continued to dart his eyes around. Stalling. He couldn't. He just couldn't. They were the good guys. We don't lose our own. We help people. We save people. I couldn't. I couldn't have. We couldn't lose one of our own.

"Err, uh," Franchise started, "we uh, we um." He took a breath and gathered himself. "We need to get back to HQ. I'll meet you two there." He received a confused nod from Hopper. Fathom looked worried. I couldn't let her down. Franchise shot a quick forced grin, then shot across the sky towards the storage facility. He found himself getting lost in thought as he zipped through the sky.

Where? Where could they have taken them? Who were they? What do they want? Did they know who she was? What she could do? Of course, they did. They have abilities, and so did she. Worth kidnapping? Who did they work for? A scowl took over his face. As he passed over the city, he was met with a scattered cheer of people that recognized him. He didn't notice. How could this happen? How could the good guys lose? He approached the front of the storage facility, slowed his pace, and stopped feet from the front door. He hit the ground straight into a step and pushed through the front door. It swung behind him and stayed open. He walked briskly through the front towards his desk. He passed Emmitt that yammered something. Franchise paid no attention as he drove forward, towards his computer. He slammed down into his seat and whirled to face the screen. He hit the power button and jerked the mouse back and forth. As the computer finally came to life, his fingers started to dance across the keyboard. He opened several different windows. News articles, police reports, tabloids, missing person's reports. He sat back in his chair and felt himself fade into the back of his mind.

Analyzing. Numbers, people, patterns. A rush of information flew past his peripherals. As highlighted "blips" flew by he would engage, categorize, understand, and refine his search. Nothing about Lingo. His fingers continued to chatter at the keyboard. Then flicked at the mouse. He repeated this motion as his eyes flew from open window to open window. His eyes widened. He sat back slowly in his chair. He started to ruffle through his desk. He rummaged and threw miscellaneous things out of drawers. He clutched at a folder and ripped it open. A list. His list. His list of potential recruits. He wasn't the only one looking.

His eyes flew to the screen again. Ripley Greggers. His fingers soar across the keyboard. Kidnapped. He flipped his list to the final pages, the more superior abilities, people that would be harder to recruit without some sort of "street cred" or reputation. The screen filled with missing person reports. Were they? Was someone? Did someone find my notes? Was someone using my list? Who? Why? Someone was taking people with abilities, and for what? They had people with abilities taking people with abilities. What sort of organization? Where were they taking them? What were they doing with them? Who's next?

Heredity. Bloodline. Abilities ran through the bloodline. Siblings, brothers, sisters, and relatives. His fingers raced over the keyboard again. Superior abilities. Some siblings were taken, others were not. Must be over the severity of abilities. Whoever these people were, they're stocking up on some pretty big firepower. These siblings taken, they're not on my list. He flipped back to the front page. He stared down at his list as he eyes widened. He tilted his head slightly.

Fathom and Hopper walked into the open area. "What's the matter?" Fathom offered.

Franchise looked up defeated, "We need to go get Gracie."

Fathom looked puzzled. She scrunched her face and asked, "Why?"

Hopper continued, "Yeah, weren't we trying to recruit her brother?" Hopper realized the fear that grew on Franchise's face as his stomach dropped. He questioned, "What is it mayne?"

Franchise grew pale as he started, "We're not the only ones recruiting."

"Like other groups?" chirped Fathom, "Like us?"

"No, Fathom. Not like us. Like those two that took Lingo," he choked out. "They're not recruiting…..they're taking. Kidnapping."

The group grew solemn. Looking at each other for answers. Growing more lost in the silence. Hopper offered, "Then why the little girl? She doesn't have any gift, does she?"

Franchise looked down a few feet in front of his boots. He mumbled, "Yes. Yes, she does."

Hopper and Fathom glance at each other. "Well," started Fathom, "what was it?"

Franchise looked up through the tops of his eyes. "Her abilities are only in their infancy. Nothing we can apply." He looked off into the corner of the room.

"Franchise… what can she do?" Hopper asked, his voice filled with concern.

"Mind control, Hopper. She has the potential to control the minds of others." Franchise muttered.

Hopper's eyes grew wide, and his jaw dropped to the ground. "And….you…uh. So, uh….some little girl can control others minds and stuff and you…uh. You took us into her house?" Hopper gained his composure. His realization grew into anger. "You put us in the same house, of a kid who can control our minds? You knew?"

Franchise looked at him with a furrowed brow and shot back, "No. Hopper. I didn't know. I met her inside. We went there for Ripley. Remember?"

Fathom looked up to Franchise with concern and spoke, "You didn't tell us?"

"No, Fathom. It wouldn't have done any good. Her mother doesn't know. And if she did, she'd be heartbroken. She lost her son. And then what? Find her daughter is…odd? A target?" Franchise's eyes grew wide again, the fog of the conversation seemed to have lifted.

"Hey, mayne!" Hopper started, "You said we're supposed to be a team! And you're holding stuff from us!"

"Hopper. There is something bigger going on!" Franchise shouted. "I have a list. A list of people with abilities. Ranked. Rated.

From useful, to super powerful. And someone else is kidnapping the useful and powerful…Hopper. My list is being used to kidnap." Franchise's eyes welled up. "Lingo is my fault."

Fathom looked up fearful and asked meekly, "Why weren't we taken?" she gestured at her and Hopper.

"You weren't on the list Fathom," Franchise muttered.

Fathom looked over at Hopper and offered, "But he was."

Hopper crossed his arms and scoffed, "Yeah Franchise, why wasn't I taken?"

"They haven't taken anyone from the bottom of the list yet," Franchise mumbled.

"Bottom? What'd you mean bottom?" scoffed Hopper. He uncrossed his arms and took a defensive stance to prove his disdain.

"On a power scale. You're near the bottom," Franchise started, "You have super strength, but it's limited. Its restricted to your lower extremities. It's limited." He looked Hopper straight into his eyes. "In the grand scheme of things, in a world of superpowers and people with abilities….you're underpowered, Hopper."

"Is that so?!" Hopper retorted as he positioned himself in Franchise's face.

"If Loner said yes, then…… we wouldn't have gotten Hopper?" Fathom meekly asked.

"I'm second string?" Hopper asked in shock towards Franchise.

Franchise tried to hold onto his composure. "We are here to protect the people. This team needs members to protect the people. Loner did not want to help. You did." Hopper grunted at the answer. Franchise jeered, "Put your feltings aside….Hero. There are people out there. Taking others. We don't know why, or what they're doing. If my hunch is right, Gracie is probably next."

"And what Franchise? I'm just supposed to forget that imma second string 'strong guy' until you find someone to replace me? Use me till I'm no longer useful?" Hopper choked out.

"No Hopper. You're still a hero. And someone needs our help," Franchise positioned himself squared up with Hopper. "Someone that can't help themselves. No one to protect them. That is why you are here. You are willing. And if you still are, we need to go get Gracie. If you don't…..someone else will. And that is what you should be concerned with, young hero." Franchise patted Hopper on the shoulder and then started to walk towards the front door. "Emmitt.

Spin up the copter. I'll meet you back at the Greggers' house." Franchise looked back and chirped, "See you two there." He picked up the pace as he pushed through the front doors. He opened into a slight jog and extended his arm. With a gentle flip of his wrist, he propelled into the air. As he whirled farther away from the storage facility, he heard the hum of the helicopter engaged behind him. A small smile grew on his face.

As Franchise drew closer to the Greggers' home, he started to scan the area. Whoever this other organization was, they could possibly be in the area. As he faded into the back of his mind, he didn't find anything out of the ordinary. He continued to fade in and out of his focus as he closed the distance to the house. He arrived at the neighborhood, and a final inspection yielded negative results. He slowed until his feet hit the ground. He walked up to the front door. No sign of forced entry. Everything looked the same as it had when they left. He knocked on the door rapidly and rang the doorbell several times. There was no response. He repeated the same sequence of events as he called out to Ms. Greggers. Franchise heard the shuffling and movement of chairs. A few moments later the door opened, and

Franchise was face to face with Ms. Greggers. She looked puzzled as her eyes met his.

"Ma'am. We need to talk," Franchise sputtered.

She started, "I'm in the middle of something right now Mr. Franchise."

"It is very important Ma'am. I have theories about your son," Franchise continued. Ms. Greggers' face lit up with some semblance of relief. She opened the door and offered for him to come in. Franchise carried on, "Yes Ma'am. It also concerns your daughter Gr......." Franchise's eyes met with the steely eyes of a young man sitting at the dining room table. He stopped in his tracks.

Ms. Greggers chimed in, "Mr. Franchise, what have you found about my son? I really am in the middle of something very important."

"Where is Gracie?" Franchise asked in a stoic tone.

Ms. Greggers remained quiet. She looked over at the man sitting at the table.

Franchise asked again. This time directed to the man sitting at the table. "Who are you? And where is Gracie?"

The man rose from his chair. "Mr. Franchise was it?" Franchise nodded in acknowledgement. "Gracie is here. She is fine and in her room. Honestly, that is why I am here." Franchise hunched forward a little and took a defensive posture, keeping an eye on the man. The man continued as he offered out his hand, "I represent SYNERGY. My friends call me Matt." The man stood about six feet tall. He wore a grey business suit on top of polished dress shoes. He had stringy wiry hair pulled back into a tight pony tail revealing a Bluetooth device in his ear. As he offered out his leather gloved hand to shake he looked over thick framed glasses. Franchise reluctantly reached out and clasped the outstretched hand. It was cold and rigid.

"What brought you here? Gracie?" Franchise asked, full of suspicion.

A smile grew on the man's face, across his chiseled jaw line. "At SYNERGY we deal in the special. The supernatural even."

"You don't say," quipped Franchise looking around at his surroundings. "So, you're here to….I don't know collect Gracie?"

The man let out a chuckle, "No no no. And that is what I was just speaking to Ms. Greggers here about. Little Gracie is special. And we can provide an environment for her to learn and understand her…specialty."

Franchise looked over his shoulder at Ms. Greggers. She had a worried looked on her face. "You say Gracie is special huh? What exactly can she do? That she would need a special environment to ....understand?"

Another chuckle from the man. "She can communicate with animals Mr. Franchise."

A bold-faced lie. Trying to gain the trust of Ms. Greggers. Smart. Similar to what Ripley could do. Gracie could also convey the same idea. Really smart.

"Does SYNERGY collect often?" Franchise probed. The grin ran off the man's face. "Perhaps earlier today? Matt?"

"What are you talking about? Collecting?" asked Ms. Greggers as she grew worried.

Franchise's eyes were fixed on the man as he explained, "People with abilities are being collected. Taken. Stolen. Kidnapped. And I think they might be the same people who took Ripley."

Her eyes grew wide, "What? What were you saying?"

"I'm saying SYNERGY is collecting people with abilities. I think they kidnapped your son. I think they're trying to take your daughter. They took a friend of mine earlier. I came to warn you. And to protect Gracie."

The man's voice grew stern, "Those are some pretty big accusations Mr. Franchise."

"The real question is what can you do? They sent two to take a woman in a wheelchair. You're only one." He tilted his head slightly as to acknowledge he knew more than what was freely given. "For someone who can.....do more than talk to animals."

The sound of a helicopter roared overhead. A smile grew on Franchise's face. The man pressed the Bluetooth on the side of his head as to acknowledge. "Yes, I know. It's under control. NO. No, I don't need any help. Don't. CHH." He made a grimace.

"So, what can you do?" Franchise asked as he faded into the back of his mind. Black. Vacant. No powers. Maybe they lay dormant like others that needed to be activated. "Hmmm. Ms. Greggers?" He called, "Get Gracie. Get her to my friends outside."

She ran towards the hallway. The man lunged in her direction. Franchise gripped his belt and with a back handed movement yelled, "BENJAMIN'S BOLAS!"

ZZZWWWITHP. The disk exploded and wrapped around the man's arms and torso. The man crinkled his face. He reached his hands across over his front and removed his gloves and let them hit the ground. He reached up and grasped the bolas. The bolas wire started to shrivel and retract. Franchise grew concerned as he faded again. The man's hands were illuminated. The bolas wasn't retracting, it was getting absorbed. All of it. Plastic from wiring fell to the ground, but the metal was being absorbed into his skin and coursing through his body. The man gave a shrug of his shoulders to show he was no longer immobilized. Franchise's eyes grew wide as he came back into focus. The man walked over to the stove and placed his hand upon it. It began to crumple and contort, and it seemed to flow into his hand leaving behind anything non-metallic. He moved his head from side to side as he cracked his neck, all that followed was the sound of metal grinding.

"What was Matt short for?" Franchise choked out.

"Mateo. Mateo Winston." He lunged forward and threw a right cross. Franchise attempted to move out of the way but was struck in the right shoulder. CLR-CHINK. Franchise flew backwards and broke through the wall next to the front door. He tumbled through the front yard screaming in agony, clutching his right shoulder.

"FRANCHISE!" Fathom screamed. She ran to his side, helping prop him up.

Franchise rose to a knee and began to bark, "GRACIE! SHE'S INSIDE. WE NEED TO…." Mateo walked through the hole ripped in the side of the house. Franchise hit his left arm on his knee. His crossbow swung over. He took aim and flicked his wrist twice. THWIP THWP. Two bolts soared through the air. TUNK TUNK. They struck the chest and abdomen of Mateo. Mateo looked down and addressed the holes put through his suit jacket. The bolts shrunk and disappeared into his body. He removed his ruined jacket and threw it into the yard. With a furrowed brow, Mateo folded in his pinky and ring finger of his right hand, imitating a gun. He pointed towards Franchise and imitated pressing his thumb down. THWIP THWIP. Two bolt shaped pieces of metal fired from his fingertips. FWWWOOOP. WAWOMP. They crumpled and hit the ground after colliding with Miles. Franchise looked up to see Fathom's hands outstretched and controlling Miles. Franchise choked out again, "We need to get Gracie!"

"On it!" Hopper exclaimed as he pushed off the ground into the air with a WOOOMP. Hopper clicked the 'H' on his chest and hovered for a moment. Mateo looked upwards and reached his palm facing Hopper. He cracked his neck again, and then extended his arm fully. Thousands of needle-like shards of metal erupted from his palm into Hopper's direction with the sound of a light machine gun.

"AH NAAWW!" Hopper screamed. He slapped his chest and collapsed his wings. He leaned back as he fell to try and shield himself with his legs. THWATATATA. THUPTHIP. "AHHHH," he screamed as barbs impaled his skin. He fell and hit the ground with a thud. The flow of metal barbs slowed to a halt. It was like a faucet being turned off. Franchise, shuddering in pain fell back into analyzing. Almost all the metal had left Mateo's body. "He's out!" he cried, "He used it all! We need to get Gracie! The time has to be now!"

Hopper slowly rose, clutching his sides. Fathom locked eyes with him, and then with Franchise. Both winced in pain. Fear took over Fathom, and she stood steadfast. Mateo stopped and pressed his finger against his Bluetooth again. "No. It is under control. I will be back shortly. No. I don't need them. Don't send them."

Hopper took this conversation as a distraction and dug in and thrust off. CRRUMPPH. Mateo turned just in time to have his chest met with a solid flexed kick from Hopper. CURTUNK. Mateo flew backward and smashed into Ms. Greggers car. The car crumpled around him.

"GO GO GO!" screamed Franchise. Hopper trotted into the house. Shortly after he emerged with Gracie in his arms. Hopper stood next to Franchise, behind Fathom and Miles. The crumpled car was almost completely gone. Only plastic, tires, leaking fuel, and a disgruntled face remained. Mateo picked up a jog in their direction. Hopper dropped Gracie next to Franchise and leapt in front of Miles. As Mateo approached, Hopper released another powerful kick. Mateo placed his arms in front of his chest and braced with one foot behind. TWANG. The metallic ring echoed. Instead of flying through the air this time, he slid backwards, creating ruts in the yard. "Uh, Franchise?" Hopper called. Mateo approached again, and Hopper tried to deliver another powerful kick. Mateo caught this one between his hands with another solid TWANG. He leaned to his left and completed several quick rotations releasing Hopper's leg and sending him flying through the air.

"Uggh," Franchise groaned. "Fathom…. Miles is going to have to help us…."

She winced, "But I….I can't."

Franchise continued, "I'm injured, Hoppers hurt….he's going to take Gracie. Just like they took Lingo. We need your help Fathom. I need your help!"

Fathom stared through Miles with tears in her eyes. Struck with fear, she stood, holding up her hands as Mateo approached.

"Fathom! You and Miles are the heroes we need! The heroes Gracie and Hopper need! You are brave and strong! We need you to hold off Mateo until I can figure this out!"

Fathom gave a firm nod. She clenched her hands into fists and gave them a slight shake. Miles emulated.

Franchise faded into analyzing. Dull blue encompassed everything. Mateo glowed from head to toe with metallic energy. A rush of information flew through Franchise's mind as he calculated the battlefield. Mateo squared up and threw a right hook into Miles. THWOMP. Miles bounced and seemed to fade into the air. Mateo closed the distance between him and Fathom. She opened her hands, and with a flash of light, Miles reappeared. She closed her fists and began to punch. DINK DINK. Miles' bulbous hands collided with the metallic man again. Mateo continued to strike back. With each strike, Fathom shuddered and grew more and more exhausted.

"Hang in there, Miles," she whispered.

Miles continued to bumble into the way of Mateo, blocking his way to Franchise and Gracie. With an uppercut from Mateo, Miles faded away again. Fathom gasped as she fell to a knee. Mateo walked in closer. Her hands open and close as Miles reappeared.

Franchise let out a defeated sigh. His analysis didn't reveal what he wanted. With the amount of metal currently absorbed, Mateo was super dense. He had also increased his weight, durability, and strength. Unless he released it, they wouldn't be able to do much against him with their current capabilities. Mateo back handed Miles once again. Miles fizzled into thin air for a final time. Fathom crumpled from exhaustion. She had never tried to use her abilities in this capacity before. As Mateo took another step closer, there was a shout in the distance. "HEY METAL MOUWF!" Hopper screamed.

A new piece to the puzzle. Franchise faded once more. There it was! With Hopper there, there was a new possibility! "HOPPER! BACK HIM UP TO THE HOUSE!" Hopper gave a nod and burst into the air. Mateo looked upwards at Hopper. Franchise loaded two more bolts into his bow. He tapped the tips of both. As Mateo raised his hand toward Hopper, Franchise launched both bolts. THWIP THWIP. Mateo looked over towards Franchise with a smug look and started to absorb the bolts again. When almost consumed, the bolts erupted with lightning tendrils. The tendrils ran up and down the course of his body locking it up, almost seizing it. "NOW, get him towards the house!" cried Franchise. Hopper descended and landed a powerful kick against the side of Mateo. Mateo slid into the remains of the car he absorbed, shaking off the results of the last bolts.

Franchise touched the tips of the two newly loaded bolts and fired both at Mateo. THWIP THWIP. Mateo caught one, and the other struck the ground next to him. He dropped it next to his feet before it could go off. He cracked his neck while staring Hopper and Franchise down.

The bolts exploded into tendrils of lightning. One caught Mateo's leg and paralyzed him in place. The other tendrils ignited the gasoline left on the driveway from the car that was absorbed. Mateo stood seizing, becoming engulfed in flames. His legs began to glow red.

Franchise loaded two more bolts, tapped the tips, and launched them, keeping Mateo seizing in flames.

A dark cloud came billowing out from behind Mateo, masking his location. Ten figures walk out of the smoke. All projections of Mirrors holding on to Ms. Greggers.

"No, no, no," whimpered Franchise.

"Oy there mate! You dint go on missin me didja?" Smoke exclaimed, peering out from the haze.

Chapter Nine: Loner

Dwarfed by the sheer size of the monstrosity in front of him, Loner took short steps backward, trying to size up Gorge. There was next to no room for this thing to move around. Approaching from the front didn't seem like the best tactic. Running straight into the door sized mouth didn't seem like a good idea. The monster clumsily clawed its way forward. Jerking its entire body, moving only slightly with each movement. Its field of vision seemed limited and it seemed to be sniffing through the air to gauge the location of its next food source. Its bottom jaw chattered and quivered as drool and remnants of its last feeding rolled out. Loner drew up cautiously, as he realized this thing was bigger than this room. It must have grown larger while in this space. And at its current size, there was no way of extracting this thing unless pieces of the building were removed. He wasn't about to free this thing, especially if it was still able to consume, grow, and become more of a threat. Loner had to find out its limits, its capabilities, range of motion. He slowly moved to one of the edges of the opening and lowered himself to pick up pieces of concrete blocks from the broken foundation.

"Alright you ugly piece of shit," started Loner, "let's saw how I can un-fuck myself here."

GRRT. Loner flexed, took aim and pegged Gorge with half a block of concrete. CRRCH. The block impacted the side of its snout, jarring its head slightly. Gorge let out a gruff snarl and rooted around as if to find where it came from.

"Fucker took it like a champ." Loner lobbed another brick at Gorge with similar results. He'll have to come from the side to avoid the massive death pit of mangled teeth and mouth parts. And then wail on the back end until it was subdued enough to be corralled by the SYNERGY dickheads like Meat. The front way wasn't going to work. Pot shots with cinderblocks weren't working nearly as well as he initially hoped for. Loner held onto his ribs and hunched over as an ache took over his body. He unflexed and took a breath. Gorge continued to snort and scramble at the ground, trying to find something to consume. Loner thought to himself: Still not a hundred percent. I really don't want to go toe to toe with this thing. Its hearty enough to take direct hits without being phased. He looked around.

There were cracks in the wall leading away from the doorway. He could just push a section of the wall and use it to avoid the mouth end of this atrocity. Kind of like a make shift dog cone. He watched Gorge continue to smack its jaws and root aimlessly. Better than punching it in the teeth. He walked over to a section of the wall and gave a heavy sigh. He placed his palms on the wall and braced with his shoulder, he laid his face against it as he took a deep breath in. GRRT. He gave a nudge forward and separated a section of wall from the building. He heard shuffling and grunts as it received attention from Gorge. Couldn't see around the wall now. Had to move before Gorge got in better position. Loner drove forward and to the left. SHRRRRRR. The cinderblock wall scraped against the floor. THUD. Loner hit resistance. He dug his feet in and drove forward. Gorge growled and roared. Loner figured he was close to the front side of the face. He needed to push past it to avoid the mouth at all costs. FOOM. Loner got kicked back a little with wall in hand. Gorge was whipping his massive head back against the wall. Loner pushed back, really digging in and forcing his way forward. Every couple of steps he was jarred backwards with another powerful blow from Gorges' head. Loner heard crumbling and cracking. He must have Gorge pinned against the wall of the building.

Gorge thrashing back and forth was literally tearing into the walls. It was about time to move. Loner went to try and push the wall forward to maneuver around to the flank when a row of giant teeth slammed down next to his face. Gorge had opened his giant maw and started to close down on the section of wall Loner had been using. Loner quickly positioned both of his hands on what seemed to be a canine tooth. Loner pushed up and back towards Gorge trying to create space. Loner struggled as the teeth continued to lower slowly. Loner pushed off the tooth and propelled himself backwards, releasing his flex. The top jaw came crashing down, pulverizing the concrete. A small cloud of debris wafted through the room. Gorge scoffed and smacked his jaws as debris fell out of his mouth. Once again, Loner was confronting the monster face to face. Loner's decision to remove a piece of the wall gave the necessary room for Gorge to maneuver a little better in its current state. Gorge used his hoof clawed hands to scuttle his massive body forwards. GROFF, NYANH, GRAWH.

GRRT. Loner flexed and propelled himself off his back foot to the right of Gorge's face. He reared back in midair as he closed the distance. As he approached, Gorge opened its gaping mouth to receive Loner. Loner connected a loaded punch into one of Gorge's teeth.

Gorge's head shifted to his right as a crack shot up his tooth. Loner's feet touched the ground, and he used this opportunity to drive off again to access Gorge's side. Gorge swung his head back and snapped his massive jaw at Loner again. Loner landed another punch on the outside of the corner of Gorge's mouth. This hit sunk Gorge into himself and sent Loner backwards. GRRT. There was distance between the two again. Loner picked up a section of the broken wall and flexed. GRRT. He pushed off to close the distance. He put both hands on the concrete block and swung it like an ax behind Gorge's left eye. It left a sizeable gash behind. Loner dropped the block and loaded up another punch and released it into the gash. Gorge bellowed in pain. Loner continued to drive punches into and around the massive wound. With each powerful hit Gorge's eye protruded more and more out of the socket. Loner grabbed onto one of Gorge's large cow like ears and started plowing punches behind it with the other hand. Gorge whipped its head back and forth and sent Loner flying. He impacted the nearby wall and soared through it. After he collided with the floor and stopped sliding, he released his flex. GRRT. His head filled with a searing pain that forced his eyes shut. It felt like someone was digging their fingernails into his ribs and pulling them inward. His kidneys felt as if they were about to burst. Every muscle began to constrict as if lightning coursed through him. Every time he exerted himself, it put more and more strain on his body. He hadn't used his ability so many times so close together. And after his near fatal run in with Terror-cane, it was clear he was not nearly in any condition to face off with this thing. He clutched at his ribs and leaned over onto his side. He pried one of his eyes open to see Gorge grunting and scuffling about, inching closer and closer. His took a breath in. It felt like fire in his lungs. Moving his head shot sparks of pain through his spine. He forced his eyes open again, Gorge still had not made very much progress. Loner closed his eyes and let the pain overcome him. He had some time before Gorge was close enough to do anything. His breathes become shorter to compensate for the burning in his chest. He let his arms fall to his side. He started to fade. A few moments go by, and Loner heard whispers and mumbling to his left.

"Shit, shit, shit, shit....shit......no no no no," the voice chattered. Loner pried an eye open and slowly turned his head towards the mumbling. It was a middle-aged woman in a lab coat. She was curled up in the fetal position rocking back and forth. Loner could see badges clipped to the pocket of her lab coat. She continued to mumble frantically under her breath, "No no no no. He was it. Now I'm going to get eaten like everyone else. Everyone else. Everyone. He can't be. He can't be dead." Loner cleared his throat. "I'm not dead," he said in a low, calm voice.

"Oh, sweet Jesus!" she cheered, "Thank fucking God. You have to get up. You have to get us out of here!"

Loner let out a groan, "Give me a minute lady." He shuttled over to his side. He winced in pain as it shuddered through his body.

"You don't looked so good," the nurse jutted.

"You don't say?" Loner shot back as he cringed.

The bumbling mass of teeth continued to scoot in their direction. Loner leaned forward and propped himself into a kneeling position. He hung his head and let the intense pain shoot through his spine.

The nurse continued to babble, "They're all gone! That thing ate everyone! I thought I was a goner. But you…..you're as strong as that thing is. You have to…..you have to save us!"

Loner continued to kneel with his eyes closed. "Did it look like that when it came to this floor?" he asked.

She looked puzzled, "Well, uh, no. Not that big…but it was big…"

"How long ago?" Loner questioned.

"What do you mean?" she chirped back.

"How long ago was it before it was this size?" he asked through gritted teeth.

CRRKKKT. CRRKKKT. The sound of stretching and tearing of leather resonated through the room. Gorge's body slumped to the ground. Its head fell limp to its side. Straps of skin split and ricocheted like rubber bands down the back of the monster. Either side of the hulking mass slumped over and splayed open. Through slimy ligaments and remnants of flesh, two shoulders arched upwards out of its back. Its torso rose upwards as its giant claw hoofed hands descended from its face.

It was reverting! It had exhausted enough energy that it couldn't sustain its current size. Its metabolism was too great, and with Loner forcing it to use its energy instead of consuming more, it had started to degrade. The monster rolled its hips, gauging its new form. Its shape resembled more human-like features but had still kept most of its beast-like form. It was half the size of its previous form. Gorge opened his eyes slowly and rotated his head from side to side. He then gave his body a violent shake like a dog to free itself from the last binding carcass. He gave a few short snorts and grunts as he reached towards the meat husk he emerged from. He clawed at it with his hoofed talons and greedily thrust it into his gaping maw. Smashing his jaws together crushing through the tough hide of his former self. Gorge's hunger was insatiable as he started to devour any flesh in sight.

Loner breathed heavily. He was beyond exhaustion. And to see Gorge reborn anew started to extinguish all hope. Loner looked out the side of his eyes to meet those of the nurse. There was little hope of staying alive if they stay. Loner gave a shake of his head to gesture for her to leave. At that moment, Gorge snapped his head upwards with meat dripping from his teeth. He gave a few gruff grunts as if to force movement again. Loner continued to breathe slowly and kept his eyes fixed on the new Gorge. Eventually, Gorge lost interest and continued to consume the husk. Loner looked back in the direction of the nurse slowly. She stayed hunched behind the wall, shuddering, shaking, convulsing, with her hands over her mouth muffling her whimpers. A high pitch squeal made it past her cupped hands. Gorges face immediately sprung up again with another gruff vocal noise. He shortly returned to his task at hand. Loner thought to himself that Gorge's vision must still be pretty poor and his primal instincts still drive his primary actions. But as the husk grew smaller and smaller, Loner felt something he hadn't felt in a long time. Fear.

Loner tried again to lock eyes with the nurse. She continued her nonsense but finally met Loner's gaze. Wide-eyed, Loner slowly lifted a single finger to his mouth. In turn, she gave a short nod of acknowledgement. Loner turned to face Gorge again. Keeping his eyes fixed on the monstrosity tearing through his former self, Loner started to inch towards the nurse. As he grew closer, Gorge slammed the remaining bits into its gaping mouth and threw its head back. It arched its back and rolled its shoulders back. Gorge slowly extended its legs and lifted itself off the ground. This time it was still mostly torso, with large muscular arms. Its mouth opened and ended midway through the chest. He had shorter legs, but that added to mobility. Gorge lowered its clawed hands to the ground, and in conjunction with its hind legs, started to turn its body around. As it laid one of its hoofed claws on the ground, he jutted his head in the air in a sniffing motion. It rocked its entire torso forward. Each snort and sniff was followed by a snapping of his bottom jaw. He stopped his movement and started to sniff intently in the air like a dog who had caught sent. His jaw chattered and clacked. Loner froze with his hands held in the air, palms towards the wall.

In a guttural growl, Gorge chattered and spat, "I'SSSS…….. CAANNN…… SMEELLLLSSS….. YOUUU…."

"Fuck," Loner muttered. Gorge's head snapped in his direction. His jaw snapped and chattered. He slowly started to turn, alternating claws and hind legs again.

"I'SSSSSS…….. CAANNN….. TASSSTESS….YOOUUU," Gorge chattered again.

The nurse let out a shrill chirp of fear and terror. Gorge snapped its torso in her direction and started to clamber towards her, snapping his jaw. He was much more mobile in this form. Half the size, and able to maneuver his body. With each of Gorge's jaw snaps and chattering the nurse let out another shrill yelp. With each yelp, he tilted his head and homed in closer to her location. Loner continued to watch. Gorge still couldn't saw. Even in a less monstrous form, he was still too animal-like. Fortunately, cows and pigs weren't known for their superb vision. Loner tried to lock eyes with the nurse again. He continuously mouthed the words, "Shut. Up." But at this point she was inconsolable. Gorge continued to chatter his bottom jaw, waving his snout from left to right. Feeling. Trying to find more. Anything, and everything.

"I'SSSS…….. WILLLL… EAATTSSS…. YOUUU……" Gorge bellowed into the darkness.

Gorge was now yards away from the nurse. He let out a gruff noise, then swiped his talons from in front of its face outwards and scraped his talons across the wall with a terrible screech. Loner drew in a few quick breathes and fixed his stance. He dug in his rear foot and put his weight back onto it. GRRT. He thrust forward as he cocked back his fist. At the sound of crushing tiles under Loner's foot, Gorge whipped his head in his direction. Loner unloaded a heavy hand into the upper jaw of the brute. Gorge's body spun and collided with the wall. Brick and dust exploded around him. The nurse erupted into a panic and began continuously screaming. Loner advanced forward to close the distance. In a moment, Gorge swung a massive backhand around and collided with Loner's torso, sending him airborne. He spun shortly and collided with the floor. He couldn't see. GRRT. Focus came back. His sunglasses were gone. Gorge scuttled forward to the left and then right, letting out growls and snaps. Loner looked around frantically for his shades. There was rubble and litter everywhere. Battling a giant mouth blind was insane. Gorge was strong. Real strong. And it could move. Loner continued his frantic search. Gorge swung a massive hoofed talon at the nearby wall, and dragged more rubble and brick, throwing it behind him. It fell all around the nurse who in turn continued to whimper and scream. Gorges snout flared, and his jaw chattered. He began to lumber and turned to face the nurse. As he clambered forward, Loner heard a distinct CRRKT. Loner let out a pitiful sigh. As Gorge's rear leg lifted into the air, Loner saw remnants of his glasses. As Gorge gained some distance, Loner followed slowly behind. He knelt and picked up his fragile frames. The left lens was completely pulverized, and the earpiece was missing. The right side, however, was intact. Better than nothing he thought to himself. He looked around frantically for some way to keep them together. Through the destruction and rubble, he manages to salvage a roll of medical tape. He quickly sat the remnants of his glasses on his face and proceeded to run the tape around his head securing the one lens over his right eye. Gorge continued to thrust his talons outward and drag them backwards hoping to catch the nurse. Loner dug into his stance and flexed again. GRRT. He sprung forward and onto Gorge's back.

Gorge rolled his shoulders and frantically whipped his arms backwards. Loner dug his fingertips into Gorges flesh and gripped into his muscles. Gorge bellowed with pain. Loner hung on as Gorge thrashed about. Loner began to climb the creature's back using the same methods while trying to maintain his flex. He finally scaled the monstrosity to its right shoulder. He gripped in deep with his left hand and loaded up his right. He began to rain down punches that hit like sledgehammers over, and over, and over again. Gorge's arm extended all the way out, then went limp. Gorge lowered his shoulder and thrust it into the nearby wall. He began to scuttle forward dragging Loner through it. Loner's flex flickered out and then back in as he let out a scream. The wall fragments dug into his soft flesh. Gorge continued to press Loner along and through the wall. Loner's flex flickered again with more intense pain. Stinging, burning, throbbing. It started to take hold over Loner. GRRT. He released his left hand. Gorge thrashed about again and sent Loner flying overhead. Loner landed with a thud and slid, stopping alongside the nurse. The light grew dim through Loner's eyes as he slowly faded out of consciousness.

"SHIT, FUCK, FUCK, FUCK, SHIT," cried the nurse, "nonononono. Come on come on come on man." She reached out and started slapping him in the face. "Come on come on come on," she repeated. Gorge lifted its right arm and rotated it around a few times.

"NOOWWSSS.....III......EEEAATTSSS......YYOOOOUU UU," Gorge chattered.

"The fuck you will," the nurse cursed with tears streaming down her face. She looked down at Loner and stated, "I'm sorry man.....but I need you." She reached down and pushed up his left sleeve. She removed a syringe marked 'EPINEPHRINE' from her pocket and removed the cap. She flicked the inside of Loner's elbow a few times, and then pushed the needle in and slammed on the plunger.

Loner's breathing picked up in pace. He started gasping at the air. In an instant, his eyes flew open, and he sat straight up. YAH. HAH. YAH. Loner barked. His arms started to pulse inward to clutch his chest. Blood started to stream from his eyes and ears. The epinephrine surged through his body, coursing, flowing, feeding it. It forced his body into a flex as every vein in his body protruded and engorged. YAH. HAH. YAH. He growled again. He frantically whipped his head back and forth to see what was going on. He was confused and overwhelmed.

"There you go," the nurse offered with a meek smile.

"WHAT. WHAT THE. FUCK?" Loner barked.

"You were out. I had to. I hit you with Epi," she informed. "We need to go. Now."

Loner tilted his head and saw Gorge. Rage filled him. He pushed himself up to a knee, then up to both feet. He felt terrible. He felt amazing. He felt powerful. He closed his fist and felt it course through his system. GAH. HAH. YAH. He squared up his shoulders and leaned forward with his arms cocked back. "RAAAAAAAH," he screamed then clenched and gritted his teeth. Gorge whipped its head forward and bellowed back, "GAAARRROOOAAAAAH."

"AAAAHHHH YOU UGLY PIECE OF SHIT," Loner screamed. He pushed off and launched himself forward. He tucked his left hand behind his left pocket and unloaded a left cross into Gorge's lower jaw. Gorge gurgled and spun around. He whipped one of his large arms to backhand Loner again. Loner dug in his rear foot and crossed his arms in front of his face. Gorge connected, and Loner slid backwards a few yards. Loner pushed off again and loaded up a right hook. He connected with Gorge's left eye. Gorge coughed, sputtered and fell forward bracing himself with his arms. Loner unloaded four more right hooks rapid fire into the temple of the monster. Gorge swung its arms outward and then in, wrapping them around Loner. He drew Loner in towards his large gaping mouth. With Gorge's hands wrapped around Loner's waist, Loner placed his feet in between teeth on the bottom jaw. Loner then placed his hands between teeth on the upper. The pressure was immense. Both jaws powered towards each other with talon hoofed claws gripping and pushing Loner into them. Loner struggled against the force as the jaws drew closer and closer together. Loner gritted his teeth, he was almost in a full squat position. He took a few quick breathes and drove as hard as he could downwards and upwards. The jaws shuttered and quaked as the two strengths fought against each other. Loner stood, arms and legs fully extended. He had a quick thought. He looked at the size and shape of the jaws, then took a deep breath. Simultaneously, he moved his hands from the roof of the mouth and dug his fingers into the meat of Gorge's forearms. He then kicked backwards off the back of the teeth of the lower jaw, into Gorge's mouth. The jaws collapsed with tremendous force and sliced through Gorge's own arms. His mouth flew open as he bellowed in agony. Loner rolled outward onto the floor. Still with Gorge's arms and hands in his grasp, he rose, then began to throw haymakers into the mutilated monster. GAH HAH

YAH GAH. Loner continued to shout as he pummeled continuously. Without his arms to support his awkward form, Gorge toppled forward. Loner walked up the snout, clasped his hands together and struck them down between the beast's eyes. Like swinging an axe, again and again until the beast laid limp. Loner walked down the snout, then screamed into Gorge's vacant eye. Loner landed a powerful kick to the side of its head to ensure Gorge was done playing.

Loner stood over this monster, taking exaggerated breathes. Suddenly it ran out. Loner could feel the ache, agony, and pain waft back into his body, starting at the base of his spine and radiating outward. He felt like his organs were going to explode. He hit both knees and closed his eyes. After a moment, he felt something grab his arm and rant in incoherent talking. He pried an eye open. It was the nurse again.

"It's time for you to leave nurse," Loner said plainly as he gestured with his hand. She squabbled some more, but Loner didn't pay any attention. He had to get to his bag to call for pick up. He released the monster's arms. They fell and flopped to the ground. He slumped to his side and started to crawl on all fours to his bag. He sat beside it for a second. Looked up at the nurse and said, "Leave. Now."

She squawked a bit, forced a hug onto Loner, and then left. Loner retrieved the phone and dialed the number. "He's ready," he muttered into the phone, pressed the button to end the call and rested his back against the wall. Every time his eyes drifted shut, he forced them to stay open, this was no time to sleep on Gorge. Not after all that.

Loner felt like he had been watching Gorge for hours when he heard commotion downstairs. Metal clacking and feet stomping up the stairs. Men flooded onto the floor, instantly skirting the walls. After ten men enter, Loner's old friend Captain Dickbag walked in behind them.

"Well if it isn't Captain Dickbag," Loner spat.

"I thought I told you last time to bring them outside," he shot back.

"This is as good as it gets. Your turn," Loner gestured a hand towards Gorge.

Captain Dickbag gave hand signals to his men. They immediately circled the incapacitated monster. They all gave each other a nod or verbal command and opened fire on the downed creature.

"The fuck?" Loner looked puzzled.

Ten shotgun shell sized cartridges stuck out of Gorge's skin. All the men stood watch as the back of Gorge started to shift and wave under the skin. THWIP. KRRRKT KRRRKT. Gorge's back split open. It was like before. As the new creature emerged, it was berated with a slew of cartridges again. It spat and winced as it hit all fours and began to shutter. A few minutes go by, and the process started over. Whatever they were hitting it with was forcing him to revert.

"What are you hitting him with?" Loner asked.

Captain Dickbag looked at Loner out of the side of his eye and gave a slight sigh. Then replied, "A metabolism stimulant." Loner gave a few nods of acknowledgement. Each beast that emerged continued to shrink in size. Finally, a human form appeared and started to gasp and plead as it was also met with a slew of cartridges. Loner raised an eyebrow as it too hit all fours and its back split down the middle. Out clambered a submissive residual being. It looked too frail to be human, gaunt and homely with sunken in eyes and protruding bone structure. Immediately, the men surrounding it hit it with tasers. It screamed and winced as they slap shackles on its hands, feet, and face.

"Load 'em up boys," Captain Dickbag announced to his men. Two of them grabbed the residual Gorge and easily picked him up and carried him off. Two men approached Loner, and he gave a nod in agreeance. He didn't know their plan, but he was thoroughly exhausted.

He allowed the two men to pick him up and carry him down the stairs. He closed his eyes and let the pain carry him away. He felt the steady bounce of each step down the stairwells. His skull ached and throbbed in and out. He felt himself placed into the back of a vehicle and heard the door slam. Every bone felt as if they were splintered, each muscle as if they had been peeled from the bone. Loner squinted hard through the pain and could feel the clots in the corners of his eyes. He felt the vehicle sway left and right as it turned. It felt as if fire had filled his lungs and run all the way through his throat and nose. He felt the vehicle stop, and he heard the back doors swing open. He was slumped over onto the floor. He felt two people grab him and drag him out. He clutched at his one lensed glasses and pulled them off his face. Loner was slung over someone's shoulder who started walking down a hallway. Loner reached down and tucked his broken shades away. He didn't need Dr. Monroe seeing them. Plus, these jackoffs won't remember him having glasses taped to his face, they were more preoccupied with a meat-eating monster. Loner felt himself being dumped onto a bed. He pried one of his eyes open to ensure he still had his satchel and then closed it again. He was back in one of

SYNERGY's sterile white rooms. He tucked his satchel under his chest and let himself fade off.

There were a few rapid knocks at the door. Loner raised his eyebrows, face down in his pillow, and gave a low groan. A few more rapid knocks occurred, followed by the clearing of a throat. Loner began to prop himself up with his elbow. Every ounce of him throbbed and pulsed with pain. He tilted his head towards the door. Dr. Monroe stood in the doorway with a scowl.

"You look terrible," Dr. Monroe spat, "not even the decency to clean up?"

Loner looked back down at his pillow. There were blood stains from his face and clothes. He looked back at Dr. Monroe and gave a faint shrug.

"Come on then," Dr. Monroe sneered.

Loner rose slowly and began to shuffle his way to the door. Dr. Monroe turned and started to pace down the hallway to the briefing room. He opened the door and held it open for Loner.

"You nearly killed the experiment," scoffed Dr. Monroe.

Loner sucked his teeth in response.

"Unacceptable. Luckily when he changes forms, he can form new limbs," Dr. Monroe sneered.

"He's here, ain't he?" Loner shot back into a frustrated look from the doctor. Loner continued, "Where's my info on my brother?"

Dr. Monroe furrowed his brow and turned to retrieve a folder. He placed it on the table and slid it over to Loner. Loner leaned over the table and grabbed it. He flung it open. There were several pictures. White male. Tall with long stringy hair. Most of his face covered either by the angle of the shot or a baseball hat. Except one. His features were the same, but all grown up. Loner's stomach sunk as he spoke, "You found him? You found him! Where is he?"

Dr. Monroe turned and retrieved another folder and slid it across the table. "Another mission," he said coldly. Loner felt himself getting physically upset. They found his brother. They knew where he was. But they won't tell him. He stared at the outside of the blank folder with a distorted grimace, "What now? What fucked up dumpster fire am I walking into this time?"

"Come now Loner; this one should be much easier. Potentially," Dr. Monroe said smugly.

Loner turned the file to read the code name: WISH. "What's a WISH?" he asked as he flipped open the file. He glanced at a picture of a teenage black girl. His heart stopped. This was the same girl who was with Franchise.

"Gorge and Meat are the results of a newer operation called Project FULCRUM. It's the application of a serum that forced evolutionary leapt. WISH was a result of a far older experiment," Dr. Monroe stated.

Loner raised an eyebrow. "This is a child," he said pointing to the picture.

"Twenty-five years ago, a virus was created for Project PROXY. Low-income housing was offered through a 'company,' and the inhabitants were subjected to the virus. This virus affected the male reproductive system. It increased the production of children born with abilities," Dr. Monroe said plainly.

"You created a baby boom of supers?" Loner asked in shock. Dr. Monroe shot back a blank stare. Loner continued, "So what is WISH?" Loner already had experienced what she could do, even if just on a small scale. He just wanted to see how honest the doctor would be.

Dr. Monroe answered, "WISH is an experiment that applies conjuration. Whatever the subject can imagine, it is possible for it to create out of thin air."

"That sounds dangerous," Loner offered.

"It is," Dr. Monroe replied.

Chapter Ten: Franchise

Franchise's heart sunk. His stomach felt as if it was being wrenched and pushed upwards into his throat. Clouds of smoke continued to billow outwards from inside and behind the house. Projections of Mirrors and Ms. Greggers pushed pass the darkness into plain view. The gaunt and greasy Australian man sauntered into view with a smile revealing his rotting teeth.

"You missed your ol' pal Smoke did'ja?" he cackled.

Franchise frantically shot his eyes about, fading in and out, trying to find an outcome, any plan of action that would permit them to escape. In the same instant, another shape pushed through the dark and looming fog.

"I told you I was taking care of it Smoke!" Mateo yelled.

"Oh, it looked like it, alright," Smoke chirped back.

This could be it. Franchise leaned forward slowly and pressed the symbol on his belt. He immediately covered it with his hand as he muffled a chirp. He tucked his chin and spoke lowly through clenched teeth, "Emmitt. Bring the chopper to my location. Hover in position. As low to the ground as possible."

"Last I checked, me an' ol' Mirrors got our last mark," Smoke pressed Mateo.

"Enough! I'll deal with your boney ass later!" Mateo sneered as he turned towards Franchise and Fathom and continued, "Let's grab the other Greggers kid and get out of here."

Smoke sucked his teeth and grabbed a new cigarette out of his vest pocket. He placed the cigarette between his teeth and leaned his face into his cupped hand and awaiting lighter flame. The tip of the cigarette glowed red as he inhaled deeply. The cherry ran down the shaft towards the filter. He flicked the butt away from him and continued to draw in breath. He puffed his chest then leaned forward and released another great cloud of dark fog. The fog spread and advanced forward, towards the young heroes. Franchise closed his eyes and wrapped his arm around Gracie and Fathom. He could hear and feel them whimpering in fear. And then a familiar rhythmic thumping. He opened his eyes to witness the smoke seeming to halt. It seemed to retreat slowly rather than rush backwards towards the house. Franchise removed his arm from around the girls and hit the symbol on his belt again. He screamed over the sounds of the helicopter blades, "EMMITT! AIM THE ROTOR WASH TOWARDS THE HOUSE!"

The helicopter chuffed overhead and kicked up debris, gravel, and sand towards the house. Smoke's fog dissipated around the house as he was thrown end over end backwards. Mirrors grabbed Mrs. Greggers and knelt trying to protect her from the incoming debris. Mateo placed his arms up to block the wind as he braced with one foot back. Franchise looked over towards Hopper who was kneeling with one of his arms up blocking sand and gravel from getting in his eyes.

"HOPPER! GRAB FATHOM. GET IN THE COPTER!" Franchise screamed at the top of his lungs as he gestured with his hand. Hopper gave a few short nods and pushed off his back foot with a flex. He appeared to glide across the ground through the whipping air. He placed his arms under Fathom's and hugged tightly. He tilted his head upwards and launched the two of them towards the helicopter. Franchise leaned his face over to Gracie's ear and shouted, "YOU NEED TO PUT YOUR ARMS AROUND MY NECK AND HOLD ON TIGHT." This was met with wide eyes from Gracie and continuous tears. Franchise grabbed one of her arms with his hand and threw it around his neck. She immediately grabbed on with her other hand and buried her face into his chest. Franchise guarded his injured arm and spoke through gritted teeth, "GRACIE. STRAIGHTEN OUT MY RIGHT ARM. UP."

She grasped at his wrist and slowly pried it upwards. Franchise spat and cursed in pain. As soon as it was fully straightened he clenched his fist and flicked it downwards. With a jerk, his boots engaged and lifted both of them into the air. They climbed slowly and advanced toward the helicopter. As he positioned himself toward the door, Hopper reached out and grabbed Gracie first, and then pulled in Franchise. "GET US OUT OF HERE EMMITT," Franchise screamed.

The helicopter swung around its tail end and quickly gained altitude. Franchise slumped against the wall and window, shuddering in pain. He did it. They did it. They saved Gracie. This was definitely a win. A win they desperately needed.

Franchise heard a gasp over the whirling rotor blades and heard Fathom mutter through cupped hands over her mouth, "Oh my God." Franchise opened his eyes to see Fathom's face pressed against the window. He turned his head and peered outwards. He looked down to see Mirrors with her arms outstretched with Mrs. Greggers crumpled on the ground behind her. Mirrors seemed to be arguing with Smoke. Smoke was yelling and jabbing his gnarled finger in her direction. Mirrors argued back. Smoke grasped at the back of his vest and drew out a jagged blade. He jutted it forward, pressing the tip at the base of Mirrors' throat. She pursed her lips and slowly moved to the side. Smoke pushed her the rest of way and grabbed a fistful of Ms. Greggers' hair and dragged her backwards. He ensured they were both facing the direction of the helicopter. With an abrupt jerk, he snapped her neck backwards exposing her neck. Smoke exposed his crooked and discolored teeth as the corners of his mouth curled into a smile. He leaned over and spoke into Ms. Greggers' ear. He rose from lurching over her and placed the handle of his knife on her left shoulder. Smoke curled his wrist inwards and dragged his hand across her neck until his arm was straightened behind him. His face became speckled in crimson droplets as he released his grasp and let the late Ms. Greggers collapse in her front yard.

Franchise felt hot breath quiver on the side of his face. He turned his head slightly to witness the quaking eyes of the young Gracie. She choked and gasped for air as tears streamed from her eyes. Fathom looked frantically from Franchise to Hopper for any semblance of reason or direction to what came next. Franchise turned his head even farther to catch the gaze of an awestricken Hopper. Concern. Fear. Franchise turned his eyes back towards Gracie. He placed his left hand on her face and offered condolences, "I'm sorry young hero. We will keep you safe from those people looking to use you, that took your brother."

Gracie looked hollow as she stared into the distance. This was too much for a child to bare. Franchise flicked his eyes around the cab of the helicopter. Hopper. Fathom. Gracie. All distraught and solemn. This was worse than losing Lingo. How was he going to keep them going? Keep them together? Keep them looking for Lingo?

No one spoke a single word the rest of the ride to the storage facility. Even after landing on the roof, everyone sat steadfast, not wanting to move on, or acknowledge what happened. Emmitt was the first, followed by Franchise. "Thank you, Emmitt," Franchise offered as he placed a hand on Emmitt's shoulder. Emmitt offered a nod. Franchise looked back into the cab and spoke purposefully, "Fathom. Hopper. Take Gracie into one of the open spaces and set her up a bed. Stay with her throughout the night. Hopper. Leave me your wings. We need upgrades."

Hopper looked confused but offered a nod. He unclasped his backpack and handed it to Franchise. He then helped Fathom and Gracie down from the helicopter and shuttled them inside. Emmitt followed, and Franchise shortly after. He walked down the hallway to his space and threw Hopper's pack onto his bed. He sat poised on his bed, slowly decompressing from the events that had happened over the past few days. What he had been through. What he had put the other members of his team through. What they were up against. Who they were up against. More pieces to the puzzle. Out matched. Almost completely. They needed more. He started to disconnect his boots and pieces of his suit and placed the components into the wheeled cart across from his bed. He called for Emmitt, and once he came, asked him to help disarm and break down Franchise's crossbow. With all the components and pieces of his weaponry in his cart, he pushed it down the hall towards a room at the end of the hallway. He flicked on the light and started to lay out the equipment on one of the countertops. He rolled back his shoulders and winced. He grabbed a spiral bound notebook and started to scribble down all the findings and outcomes from the past few days. Flaws. Advantages. Disadvantages. Shortcomings. He tore out each page and taped them to the wall above his laid-out equipment. Finally, he dragged a chair into the middle of the room and fell into it. Facing his preparation. He began to focus and faded into the back of his mind. His mind flew through possibilities and solutions highlighting components and equipment. He faded back into his own mindset and approached the work bench. Welding, clanking, and power tools echoed down the hallway throughout the night as he lost himself in his work.

The next morning Hopper slinked down the hallway to see Franchise continuing to work on Hopper's wings. "Still working, huh?" Hopper pried.

Franchise held out his hand and pointed to the opposite side of the bench without looking up from the pack. "Can you hand me those fuses over there?" Franchise said plainly.

Hopper walked over and picked up the package, handing them to Franchise. "So what'cha workin on?" Hopper asked.

"Upgrades. Our equipment was….cute. But barely functional." Franchise said coldly. Hopper squinted and curled the corner of his mouth. Franchise continued, "I'm almost finished with your pack." He placed a few fuses in place and then closed the compartment. He flipped over the pack to expose the straps and symbol on the buckle.

"Originally, this was the only way for you to open and retract your wings," Franchise said pointing to the 'H' in the center. "It was selfish and stupid of me to construct equipment like that. More of a novelty than anything else. Now you'll be able to open and close them by pressing these different locations. Also, there's a quick release function to ensure you can drop it or get out of it when you need to. You have a spotlight now built into the top." Franchise pointed to the new upgrade placed and pressed on the top exposing the new spotlight.

Hopper gave an impressed smile and patted Franchise on the back. He started, "You weren't up all night workin on my pack were ya?"

"No," Franchise stated plainly, "I had to fix the toys on my equipment."

"Toys?" Hopper asked with a smirk.

"Yes. Once again, novelties. Stupid poses to engage my equipment. Obviously exposed wires. Not functional."

"Yesterday was pretty real mayne," Hopper said with concern.

"I know," Franchise replied coldly, "this wasn't what I imagined at all. There are so many people in our city. In our state. In our country, world even. So many with the ability to help, with power to protect others. And barely any do. And now this SYNERGY. I can barely get people on our side, and they're kidnapping those who can help. And even the helpless." Franchise trailed off and stared into the corner.

"What are we going to do about Gracie?" Hopper asked.

"I don't know Hopper. We have to protect her. She is too….." Franchise trailed off again.

"She's a kid man. Who lost her brother. That just watched her mom die," Hopper said sternly.

Franchise looked him in the eye, "She can control minds, Hopper. She doesn't know how yet. But she will. Whatever SYNERGY wants. Whatever they want to do. We can't let them get her."

"So, we sit in an old storage building? Until what mayne?" Hopper asked.

Franchise took in a short breath and changed the topic. "How is Fathom?"

"She's as shook up as Gracie," Hopper answered.

"How's your ribs?" Franchise asked plainly.

"About as good as your arm and shoulder," Hopper chuckled back.

Emmitt entered into the room with a puzzled looked on his face, "Hey, Mr. Martinez. There are some people at the front door looking for you?"

Franchise and Hopper's faces went blank. Franchise threw Hopper his pack and frantically screwed and fastened components of his suit back together. Hopper helped to seat the crossbow back onto Franchise's arm, then slipped his boots on. "Emmitt, stay with the girls. Bring your radio. If I call you, take them in the helicopter and leave. Go anywhere," Franchise instructed. He and Hopper cautiously paced towards the front of the building. They were in no shape to defend their base. They would only be a mild distraction. Barely a speed bump. Hopefully, it would be enough.

Franchise and Hopper stood on either side of the front door locking eyes with each other, awaiting a signal. Franchise pumped his left arm backwards, and the crossbow swung into place. Franchise positioned himself dead in front of the door with his left arm fully extended and gave Hopper a nod. Hopper jerked the door and swung it open.

In the doorway stood a short-statured balding man with thick glasses and a bulbous nose. The man's eyes met with the extended crossbow arm, and his arms shot immediately into the air to show he was unarmed.

"WHO WERE YOU?" demanded Franchise.

"B-b-b-b-barn-a-b-b-y!" he sputtered back.

"Barnaby?" Hopper repeated with a cocked eyebrow.

"Yeah. He's with me," Loner said as he pushed into view. His eyes darted towards Franchise's extended arm. "You pop me with that thing again, and we're going to have issues."

Franchise dropped his arm. He asked with a puzzled face, "What are you doing here?"

"We got some things to talk about," Loner said as he looked up at Hopper. He offered a gentle nod to acknowledge.

"Well, we could use you right about now. Things have come up, and we could use your help," Franchise said with a bit of relief.

"Look kid, I'm still not interested in your after-school special superhero club," Loner said coldly as he looked left and right over his shoulders. He continued, "Can we come in?"

Franchise cocked an eyebrow and pointed at Barnaby, "Who's that?"

"Barnaby the eye doctor. Who's that?" Loner said pointing at Hopper.

"Hopper. Your replacement," Hopper shot back smugly.

Loner looked Hopper in the eye and responded, "adorable." He looked back at Franchise and continued, "Now that we got that out of the way, can we come in now?"

Franchise gave a nod and gestured with his head to come in. He turned and lead them towards the open bay with chairs and tables. "Why are ya'll half dressed?" Loner began to ask, "Ya'll get down like that?"

Franchise tried to offer up a chuckle but was too drained. "It's been a crazy couple of days Loner," he offered.

"I know the feeling," Loner responded. Franchise and Loner finally faced each other and took in the severity of their current conditions. "You look like shit," he told Franchise.

"Have you seen your face?" Franchise retorted. Loner scoffed in response.

Loner stated, "You should let Barnaby take a look at you guys while he's here. He's not a real doctor," he paused to look at Barnaby, "But he could patch ya'll up in the meantime." Franchise closed his eyes and nodded. He offered a thank you. Loner looked around, visually scouting the place out. "Where's the girl at?" he asked Franchise.

Concern grew on Franchise's and Hopper's faces. "Which girl?" Hopper probed.

"What do you mean which girl? You recruited more?" Loner asked suspiciously.

A wave of relief lifted from Franchise's shoulders. He responded, "Fathom? She's here. She's taking some downtime to cool down."

"Anybody been around lately? Looking for her?" Loner pried.

Franchise shook his weary head. "No, she's been with us," he said motioning from him to Hopper.

"There are people looking for her man," Loner stated.

Concern moved back across Franchise's face. "What are you talking about?" he asked sternly.

"I've been doing a few jobs for this guy. He's been tracking down particular, quote, unquote, experiments," Loner offered, signaling with his fingers. "Big, bad, ugly mother fuckers. Real nasty shit heads. After the last job, they handed me this," Loner said as he handed over the file marked WISH. Franchise gripped the file, threw it on the desk. He flipped it open and instantly faded back into analyzing. No new information was revealed. He instantly sat in his computer chair and started clicking away at the keyboard. Nothing of relevance.

"What else?" Franchise barked. "What else do you.... these people know about her?"

Loner stayed calm and stated, "Apparently there was an entire generational trial for the experiment PROXY. They say her abilities resulted from it."

Franchise returned to the computer screen and started rapidly imputing information and analyzing and refining his searches. There was no public information on Fathom or the PROXY experiments. As he continued to frantically search through data, he purposely faded back to reality. He turned to Loner and asked sternly, "Who is THEY?"

"They call themselves SYNERGY," Loner said sarcastically.

Franchise's stomach instantly knotted and rolled. He shut his eyes tight and bowed his head. He asked in disbelief, "They call themselves what?"

"SYNERGY," Loner stated again. The name rang through Franchise's head as he felt himself grow physically sick.

"Ain't that th--?" Hopper started to ask.

"Yes," Franchise snapped as he pressed his hands into his eyes and began to gently rub them with small circles. He breathed in and out deeply. "This isn't good," Franchise dragged out, "we have run into a few people that have been working for them. They have kidnapped some of the people I have been trying to recruit. We actually caught them in the act. Twice."

Loner cocked an eyebrow and asked, "What kind of …..them?"

"One could manipulate air molecules. The other one could make projections of herself," Franchise stated plainly.

"And Metal Mowf," Hopper chipped in, "dat guys crazy."

Loner looked at Franchise, "What's a Metal Mouth?" he asked.

Franchise took a deep breath in and decided to withhold some of the truth for now. He began, "One of their procurers they send to acquire new talents."

Loner seemed content with the answer. "These guys are pretty serious. They got a lot at their disposal. And some of their experiments are ruthless," he said, "I guess you guys got pretty lucky."

"I don't know mayne," Hopper butted in again, "Metal Mowf almost did us in." This was met by another cocked eyebrow from Loner. Hopper continued, "Yeah, that's why we look like this." He gestured down at his and Franchise's attire.

A grimace grew on Franchise's face. He knew more questions were coming. Loner went to speak, and Franchise cut him off, "You said you collected some of the experiments, right?" Loner nodded his head in agreeance. "What did you do once you found them?"

"Beat them down. Then called in one of their special teams to come pick them up. We'd all ride back, and I'd pick up another file," Loner stated.

"You'd ride back?" Franchise asked tilting his head, "Where?"

Loner looked around like there was a joke he wasn't getting. He returned to eye contact with Franchise and spoke the words clearly, "To SYNERGY."

Franchise's eyes grew wide, "You know where they are?" Loner responded with a few sarcastic nods. Franchise addressed Hopper in an excited tone, "We can finally rescue Lingo!"

Loner choked on a laugh, "No man. You don't want to go in there. It's intense. Cronies all over the place. Some type of technology. Not to mention the big bads I already brought back there. It is no place for kids." Hopper postured up at being called a kid. Loner continued, "Plus they want your girl anyways."

"They have one of ours Loner," Franchise said hopefully.

"That sucks," Loner said coldly, "I did my part. My good deed." Loner looked at Barnaby and continued, "Second good deed. I got what I needed out of SYNERGY. I know enough that I don't want to keep messing around with what they got cooking."

"You know the layout of their building?" Franchise asked. Loner offered a few smug nods, and responded, "Enough of it."

"Could you describe it to me?" Franchise pried.

"I'll tell you what man," Loner started out, "Me and Barnaby need to lay low for a couple of days, figure out our next move, get the fuck out of dodge. Let us chill here till we figure our shit out, and I'll even draw you a fucking map." Franchise cracked a smile and responded, "Perfect."

The next three days, Loner and Barnaby set up their areas and sat down with the other people in the building. Loner and Franchise discussed the bouts between Meat, Terror- cane, and Gorge. Loner explained the relationship of his traveling partner, Barnaby. Franchise talked about his recruiting process and the realization of his list being used. He talked about losing Lingo and the inconvenience of Smoke and Mirrors. He explained the current mood and the cause and effect of the late Ms. Greggers on the group. Gracie and Fathom were still shell shocked from the days past but began to integrate back in with the others.

On a lazy afternoon, Loner laid sprawled out on an old couch as Fathom conjured Miles and danced quietly to soft music in the background. "Is he all you can make?" Loner prodded innocently.

"No," Fathom said without missing a step. Miles followed every movement effortlessly in unison.

"What else can you make?" Loner pried a little deeper.

"Mhmmmm. I don't know," she said with a twirl, "anything I could think of, really."

"Then why...... him?" Loner inquired trying to avoid offending the young girl.

Fathom stopped in her tracks and turned to looked at Miles. She shrugged, and Miles imitated. "He's my best friend. He can always be there when I need him." With that, she went back into her rhythmic dancing with Miles.

Loner sat up and started looking around the large room. There were still clusters of boxes littered around the edges of the room. He lifted himself off the couch and made his way to a half-opened box labeled TOYS in black permanent marker. He tore the box the rest of the way open and started rummaging through its contents. He lifted up an old classic robot toy with blocky pincer-grip claws, blocky rigid legs, buttons and lights on its chest, and a single antenna sticking out of its head.

"Hey kiddo," he started, "humor me a little, won't you? Could you make that guy look like this?"

Loner held the toy out in one of his hands. Fathom stopped her dancing and pursed her mouth to one side. She outstretched her fingers and wriggled them in one at a time as Miles dissipated behind her. She stretched out her arms and held it. It looked like a cat stretching when it first wakes from a nap. She released her stretch with a heavy sigh, then locked her eyes on the toy and outstretched her hands and fingers as they began to glow a mystic blue. A swirl of the same color appeared before her and stretched upwards and downwards fabricating the image of the forgotten toy. Down to the blocked feet and the tip of the antenna, the image was a perfect replica in the dull transparent blue. She retracted her arms into her body and looked to Loner for approval. "Nice. Good job kiddo," Loner approved. Fathom shot back a goofy grin and commenced her dancing with the more rigid version of Miles.

"MITTENS!" echoed through the building. Loner scrambled to his feet and ran towards the door to see. Fathom dissipated Miles and followed closely behind. There, in the middle of the room, sat Gracie on her knees tightly hugging a small cat. Franchise and Hopper ran in from a different room.

"What is it, Gracie?" Franchise called out.

"Mittens! She's here! She just walked in!" Gracie squeaked.

"Mittens? Your cat?" Franchise asked with a puzzled look on his face. Gracie nodded forcefully, grinning from ear to ear. Franchise felt something press against his leg. He looked down to see a cat that looked identical to Mittens rub up against him. He looked up to see other identical cats scamper in from all other doorways. His eyes widened.

"Gracie! Come to me now!" Franchise yelled as dark clouds of thick smoke billowed in from each doorway.

Chapter Eleven: Loner

The rooms filled with thick black smoke. Loner covered his mouth and nose as he pried his eyes open to try to make sense of what was going on. He choked and sputtered as the thick cigarette smoke dominated the space in the rooms. His eyes burned as he quickly surveyed his surroundings. He heard muffled coughs, yelling, and increasing commotion.

"GR…ACIE!" Franchise sputtered, "WHERE…..WHERE ARE…..YOU?"

Loner swung his arm behind him. He gently collided with a body. He asked muffled through his hand, "Kiddo? Is that you?"

Fathom coughed and sputtered, "Yes."

Loner grabbed on to her arm and said sternly, "Stick with me kiddo, hold on. FRANCHISE. YOU NEED TO GET EVERYONE OUTSIDE."

"GRA…ACIE! WHERE…WHERE IS …SHE," Franchise sputtered again.

"Kid, what's the quickest way out?" Loner asked Fathom. She coughed and choked as she pointed past him. He started trudging forward through the thick smoke. He bumped into another body. "Who's this?" he spat. He reached out and grabbed a pudgy arm in a long sleeve shirt. The individual was huffing, puffing, and hacking on the smoke. They weren't answering. It had to be Barnaby. "Get up. Grab onto me." Loner felt a tug as a heavy weight pulled itself up, still gasping for clean air. He felt a pudgy hand grab at his jacket. Loner continued to push forward. He ran forehead first into the wall in front of him. His teeth clashed together as he blurted out, "FUCK." He pushed both of his hands, Fathom, and Barnaby behind him. He placed his left hand on the wall and cocked back his right. GRRT. He unloaded his fist into the wall. Bits of concrete and fragments of the wall propelled in all directions away from his fist. Light peered in as the thick smoke flowed through the opening outside. Loner placed his hands on the edges of the opening and pushed outward, making an opening even Barnaby could fit through. GRRT. Loner looked behind him as the bright sun's rays cut through the dense cloud of smog. Fathom and Barnaby stumbled forward, gasping at the clean air outside. Loner pulled them out and called back inside, "FRANCHISE, THIS WAY!"

Franchise and Hopper lumbered through the fog, choking on the fumes. Franchise pulled on Hopper's arm. "GO!" he choked out, "Into the air! Find where they have Gracie!"

Hopper nodded and thrust himself into the air. The concrete under him splintered and cratered. After a few seconds, he landed, pivoted directions, and then leapt into the air. Without his suit on, he couldn't hover or coast in the air. He repeated this process two more times. "They're on foot! They're heading to the fairgrounds!" he rattled off.

Franchise retorted, "Grab your gear! Fathom! Find Emmitt! Then we're off!" He trotted off into the building again. Hopper and Fathom quickly followed after. Loner looked at Barnaby and told him to stay put, then followed the others into the building. He approached a shaken Franchise.

"Where are you going?" Loner growled.

"After Gracie. The fairgrounds," Franchise spat back.

"Into what? Against what? These guys came into your home! What do expect to happen if you get her back?" Loner yelled.

"We're not losing another Loner! We won't!" Franchise belted back.

"Even after I painted the most vivid of pictures, you still don't know what you're up against! This is fucking stupid man!" Loner said, posturing up.

"You don't understand Loner," Franchise choked out on short breathes. "Mateo. He's…. SYNERGY has Mateo."

Loner's face grew stern and he squared up, bringing his face inches away from Franchise's. "What do you mean? SYNERGY has Mateo?"

Franchise sputtered and coughed. "We have to go Loner. They took two of ours. They have Mateo. We need to save Gracie. NOW. I don't know what they're going to try. But it can't be good. Not after what you told me. You need to come with us Loner. We're…. we're not strong enough. If it's just Smoke and Mirrors, we should be ok. But if there is anyone…anything else…. We're going to lose. Lose Gracie. We already lost Lingo."

Loner grew impatient. "You knew about Mateo? And you didn't say a goddamn word?"

"Loner, it's complicated," Franchise said as Loner grabbed him by the throat.

"Make it uncomplicated," Loner gruffed.

"The girl......," Franchise choked out, "She's.......she's .....mind...control...."

Loner released his grip and Franchise choked and clutched his throat. "What the fuck man?" Loner said in a low tone. "What were you thinking? Keeping her here?" He waved at the run-down storage facility. "These guys aren't amateurs dude! They bugged my shit! If they could track me, they could find your dumb ass broadcasting every movement on the fucking news!" He paused momentarily and looked up with a grim tone. "Fucking FULCRUM man."

Franchise shook his head left and right, "What's that?"

"It's what made the big bads. It forced evolution. Bad news," he paused, "for the kid. Not good..."

Hopper and Fathom emerged from the hole in the building. Hopper was still fumbling with his pack and Fathom was struggling to put one of her gloves on. Franchise looked Loner dead in his eyes and began, "I'm grabbing my gear, then we're going after Gracie. I want you to come with us. We will help you get Mateo back. I promise." He paused for a moment and then turned to jaunt inside the facility.

Loner looked over to Hopper and Fathom. They looked scared and worried. "They're only kids," he mumbled to himself. They were going regardless of what he said or did. These two seemed like they would follow Franchise no matter what, without fault. If Meat, Terror-cane, or Gorge were there, these kids were sure to be killed. Or captured. Subjected to FULCRUM. Franchise was going to take this girl to SYNERGY regardless to save the other little girl, even knowing they wanted her too. He was blind with tunnel vision. Loner knew he could leave. Pursue SYNERGY on his own, knowing a couple of their cronies were occupied, try to find his brother inside SYNERGY. Or he could travel with the young ones and try to ensure they didn't die. His face drooped in disgust at his options. Franchise emerged shortly after, tightening down brackets on his arm and securing his goggles onto his face. The thundering of helicopter blades resonated through the air. His helicopter shifted into view as a ladder tumbled down from above. Franchise looked at his team and gave a concerned nod. His thrusters engaged, and he propelled upward. Hopper dug in and bounded into the air. Fathom started to climb the ladder into the helicopter. Loner stood and watched the three.

He turned his head and yelled over his shoulder, "BARNABY! STAY HERE AND WATCH MY SHIT." His shout was met with confused rapid nods. As the ladder rose into the air, the helicopter lifted higher. Loner grabbed onto the bottom step of the ladder.

He made his way into the helicopter and situated himself next to Fathom. She had a fixed, distant look drawn on her face. Loner leaned over and spoke, "Stay close to me kiddo."

She looked up with concern, "Thanks for coming Loner." He acknowledged with a few reluctant nods. She continued, "I hope the metal man isn't there this time."

Loner turned his head to face her. "Metal Mowf?" he asked in his best Hopper impression. She nodded meekly. "He was scary." She looked out the window. "We're getting close to the fairgrounds," she added.

"What's a Metal mouth?" Loner pried gently.

"He's the one that tried to take Gracie. He's really strong. He was able to….," she paused and made movements with her hands trying to come up with the words, "eat metal?"

"Great," Loner scoffed as he returned to a neutral position. "Another thing that ea......."

In mid-sentence, the screeching sound of metal on metal roared through the helicopter as it tore apart. As Loner turned his head, he caught a look of sheer panic and fear strike Fathom's face. As he slowly turned his head towards the rear of the helicopter, he realized the tail end had been separated and the front was taking a nose dive, pummeling to the ground. Loner stood and grabbed Fathom under her arm. As gravity pushed against them, he drove forward to the rear opening in the helicopter. He grabbed the torn edges at the end and peered out. Large portions of metal were punctured and stuck to the sides. "THE FUCK HAPPENED," Loner screamed. The helicopter continued to tumble through the air towards the ground. Loner turned and grabbed Fathom under both arms and held her tight against his body. "HOLD ON KIDDO," he screamed. GRRT. He bent his knees and dove into the air. Further up and up he glided as he saw the front half of the helicopter continue to plummet.

"EMMITT!" Fathom shrieked.

"KID, we got bigger problems," Loner said sternly. "Hey, you remember the toy robot?"

As they sailed through the air Fathom gave a fearful nod in acknowledgement. "Alright kid, you need to make one of those goofy blue things again. You understand? Something that can fly. Alright, kid?"

She looked up with concerned eyes and stretched out her hands around Loner's body. As she began to focus, the impact of the helicopter on the ground below echoed through the air. Fathom started to incoherently scream at the top of her lungs.

"KKIIIIIDDDDD!!!!" Loner screamed into her face. "BIRD. AIRPLANE. SOMETHING WITH FUCKING WINGS!" Her eyes grew wide as her body began to shudder. She lost control of her body as she fell into shock. Loner began to look around frantically. The ground drew closer and closer by the second. He closed his eyes and embraced the trembling child. He felt the wind whip past his face. He drew in slow, deliberate breathes. And waited for impact.

WHUMPF. His entire body suddenly stopped as arms wrapped around his back. CASHINK. He felt his and Fathom's weight shift and point towards the ground. Loner opened his eyes and looked over his shoulder. Hopper's worried face met his gaze. Loner let out a sigh of relief.

"Bad news mayne," Hopper sputtered, "these wings ain't gonna hold us all." The wings on his pack shuttered and fluttered as their weight dragged them through the air. "Take the girl," Loner spat, "come back for my ass." Loner turned and pressed off with one arm and placed Fathom firmly in Hopper's arms. Hopper retracted his wings to allow for quicker decent and reopened them periodically until he placed Fathom on the ground. He propelled back into the air and secured Loner. "What the fuck happened?" Loner questioned.

"Metal Mowf," Hopper said coldly. "He shot some stuff at the chopper. We couldn't get to it soon enough."

They landed on the ground near Fathom. Loner scooped her up into his arms, then he and Hopper picked up a jog into the fair grounds. "Where is Franchise?" Loner barked.

Hopper shrugged his shoulders. "He went after Smoke and Mirrors. They had Gracie. Then the metal dude showed up," he said.

"This one ain't going to make it. She's shaken up bad. You need to find Franchise. Try to get the little girl, and we'll get out of here," Loner instructed. Hopper nodded and sprung into the air. Loner continued a quick pace down the streets of the grounds. He found an abandoned game booth and placed Fathom inside of it. "That'll have to do for now," he said softly.

"Loner is it?" echoed a cold tone over his shoulder. Loner turned to investigate this new voice. He was met with a slender man in dress pants with suspenders. He continued, "Good, you got her." He pressed the Bluetooth in his ear and spoke, "Loner has the conjurer. Smoke and Mirrors have the Greggers girl. Send escorts now. Loner and I will take care of the other two." He pressed the Bluetooth again to end the call. "Those other two are incompetent. I'm glad you're here. I've heard of your work. We'll make short work of the green and orange ones and bring these two back to base."

Loner paused for a moment and studied this man's face. Eerie. Familiar. He pried, "And who are you, guy?"

The man cracked a smile and stated, "I'm the boss's son." He walked forward and offered Loner a handshake. Hesitantly, Loner reached out and embraced the open hand. His hand was cold, stiff, and heavy. With caution, he pried again, "I'm sorry, I didn't catch your name."

"Mateo," he said with a smile.

Loner's heart sunk into his stomach as it wrenched into knots. It couldn't be. The tall, slender man couldn't be. His hands were so cold and rigid. Loner cocked his head and tried to remember the face of his younger brother. His face sunk into sadness as he remembered the subtle corners of his eyes and the way he would only smile with half of his mouth. The corners of Loner's mouth quivered as an array of emotions swarmed him. He gripped Mateo's hand rigidly and pulled him in tightly and embraced his brother in a firm hug.

"What are you doing?" Mateo asked plainly not expecting or understanding the gesture.

Loner pressed back with his hands on his brother's shoulders. "How?....When?....Why?" Loner began to gurgle out his questions through squinted eyes of disbelief.

"I could see why Dad put you on solo missions. You're pretty odd. At least you have the muscle we need. Come on, let's go get the other girl. Pick up will be here soon," Mateo said as he tried to turn. Loner gripped his shirt tightly and didn't allow him to step away. Mateo's demeanor changed as he looked at the clenched fist gripping his shirt. "Let go. Now," he said as his piercing eyes rose to meet Loner's.

"Mateo……... it's been……...years," Loner choked out, "you've…….you're so tall……"

Mateo's eyes darted from his shoulder to Loner's eyes again. His face grew stern as he sucked his teeth. He rolled his shoulders, and with a quick jerk, he landed a backhand against Loner's chin. TINK, the metallic sound echoed. Unprepared, Loner was sent airborne, spiraling into the air until he hit the nearby ground and skid.

"Hmph. Not as tough as the stories," Mateo said in a 'in a matter of fact' tone. "Bit of advice Loner, don't touch the boss's kid. Don't touch me again. Now get up. We have work to do."

Loner's head was ringing as he scrambled to his feet. "Mateo….you were just a kid, "he muttered.

"What was that?" Mateo shot back. He began to approach Loner in a quickened pace. "I told you to get up! Or would you like to stay on the ground?" He said as he landed a right cross on Loner's chin. TINK. Dazed, Loner spat blood on the ground in front of him.

"You don't understand," Loner coughed. He rose to his feet and grabbed Mateo by the shoulders and brought his face to Mateo's. "Mateo, it's me….. Frankie," Loner stated with hope in his voice.

Mateo continued his cold, distant stare. He ripped his arm up and across his chest to break Loner's grip. He leaned into his shoulder and followed through with another backhand. Before impact, Loner flexed. GRRT. He threw his hands in front of his face as they impacted. TINK. He slid backwards ten feet.

"I told you once," Mateo started.

"It's Frank. Franklin. It's me….Frankie!" Loner pleaded.

"You're grabby Frank," Mateo said looking at his shirt. "I don't like that." Mateo marched towards Loner, "I don't care if we got off on the right or wrong foot. Pick up that girl, and I'll get the other. The boss will figure out what to do with you."

"Matty….please….."

"I told you…..PICK UP THE GIRL. Transport will be here soon. And they'll bring them back to Dr. Monroe."

"No," Loner growled.

Mateo grimaced. "I don't think I heard you correctly, you weird fuck. What did you say?"

"No. I said no Matty," Loner said in a low tone.

"Why the fuck are you calling me Matty?"

"I don't know what happened to you. But I have seen the shit that has come out of that fucked up factory. These are just kids. It's wrong. What did they do to you?" Loner questioned in a low growl.

"Me?" Mateo started, "Done to me? I was rescued. This?" He said, looking at the back of his hands, "I was born like this, and Dad…..he's been very…..supportive. But that's beside the point Loner. You will pick up that girl. Because you're getting fucking paid to. And when we get back…..because of your current actions….maybe Monroe will test on you next. Now PICK UP THE GIRL!"

"No," Loner said once again in a low tone.

Mateo pressed the Bluetooth in his ear, "We got another problem here. Ensure pickup has an equalizer." He turned to ignore Loner and paced towards Fathoms location. Loner's mind raced. His brother wasn't in a mindset to listen. And if he didn't protect Fathom from him, or SYNERGY, she would be experimented on and used. But if he protected Fathom, he didn't know the next time he would see his brother. And after all these years, he was finally standing in front of him. He stood shuddering while his moral compass shook. Pain continued to sting behind his eyes. Mateo closed his distance on Fathom, and with a flick of his wrist sent the booth she was sheltered behind into the air. As he reached down to grab her, he heard the sound of leather being stretched thin. GRRT. Mateo turned to investigate and was met with an open palm, upper cutting the middle of his chest. Mateo soared through the air and crashed through the top of a nearby booth.

Tears ran down Loner's face as he fully realized the decision he had made. He had scoured high and low for ten years to find his brother. And he chose a child he barely knew over him. All the missions he did for SYNERGY, just to find him. And he was there the entire time. His face furrowed in anger. He was there the entire time. He marched towards Mateo's location. The rubble surrounding him started to rattle and shake. It started to collapse.

"TEN YEARS! TEN YEARS I LOOKED FOR YOU," Loner screamed through his teeth. "NO ONE ELSE LOOKED FOR YOU. EVERYONE. EVERYONE LET YOU GO. BUT NOT ME. Not me Matty."

Mateo rose out of the rubble and cracked his neck from side to side and then said over his shoulder, "My name isn't Matty." He raised his hand with his palm directed towards Loner. He curled his fingers backwards, and thousands of needles erupted from his palm. Loner's eyes widened. GRRT. He quickly flexed and crossed his arms in front of his face and glasses. The needles pierced his clothing and crumpled against his skin. He picked up a jog towards his brother. The stream of needles slowly dissipated until they finally halted. Mateo looked around quickly and darted towards the limits of the fairgrounds. Loner quickened his pace and followed. Mateo outstretched his hands and ran his fingertips against the chain link fence. The metal seemed to liquify and flow into his fingertips. As he moved down the length of the fence, he appeared to have consumed it all but bits of plastic. He turned and planted his feet and waited for Loner. Loner slowed his pace and came to a halt about fifty feet away from his brother.

Mateo's back faced a concrete wall, and yet he still smirked and offered a smug chuckle. Loner breathed in and out deeply as he advanced. Mateo leaned into a jog, bounding forward. Loner followed his brother's example. Loner and Mateo cocked back a fist simultaneously, but Mateo thrust his fist forward first, releasing it to expose his palm. As his fingers spread, a chain link fence net erupted from them. Loner rose his right forearm to block this. It impacted and instantly wrapped itself around his torso, pinning his arms against himself. He pressed his arms outward and shattered the chain link around him. Mateo took advantage of this distraction and landed a steely fist into the side of Loner's neck. TINK.

Loner crumpled to a knee. He attempted to load up an uppercut when he was hit with several well landed strikes. Loner pushed off the ground and distanced himself enough to gain composure. He squared his shoulders and closed the distance. TINK, TINK. He soaked up two solid punches, then landed a left hook of his own into Mateo's ribs. Mateo slid ten feet and howled in agony, folding to his side. Loner closed the distance again. TINK, TINK. Loner soaked up more of Mateo's punches, ducked under the third, and landed a straight right to the bridge of Mateo's nose. Mateo's head snapped back as he dug his toes in and slid backwards, letting out another guttural howl.

"So new daddy didn't teach you how to box, huh?" Loner goaded.

In a rage, Mateo screamed and cupped his hands together and made metallic needles erupt from the palms of his hands. Loner crossed his arms over his face and charged towards his brother. Needles impacted and ricocheted away as Loner barreled in. Mid-step, feet away from Mateo, Loner changed his foot and planted his rear foot. He dug down and threw an uppercut, landing under Mateo's ribs. Mateo's scream in agony grew fainter as he flew through the air into the distance. Loner grew solemn.

"I'm sorry Matty," he said sadly as he watched Mateo barrel into the stagnant carousel in the corner of the fairgrounds.

Loner's eyes darted around to find Fathom. She was still laying on the ground where she was placed. GRRT. Loner released his flex and cringed as he shut his eyes tightly. His sides felt like they were going to explode, and his brain felt scrambled. He pried his eyes open and walked slowly towards Fathom. As he knelt to pick her up, loud noises echoed through the fairground as if at a construction site. Scraping and clanging of metal and giant beams collapsing towards the ground. Loner tilted his head towards the carousel. It seemed to be sinking and crumpling in on itself. Levels dropped and shifted in, then fell towards the ground. Metal twisted and swarmed in and towards the middle as if it was being drawn into something. Loner pushed himself off one knee and stood. It was mesmerizing. He reached in his back, right pocket and retrieved his pack of cigarettes. Pressed one into his lips and started to shamble towards it. He sparked his lighter and drew in, igniting the tip. He took a deep drag and continued to watch the carousel in awe. Segments continued to crumble and shift inwards. As the dust settled, the silhouette of a man stood in the middle. The shape turned and started to advance in Loner's direction. With each step, the sound of metal grinding on gravel echoed through the fairground. TUR-CLINK. TUR-CLINK. Loner drew on his cigarette and stood in place. Mateo emerged from the dust cloud and clenched his fists. The sound of metal grinding on metal resonated.

"You ain't getting the girl, kid," Loner said plainly.

Sheets of metal rose out of Mateo's skin and curved to form segments of plating over his shoulders, arms, and legs. Sheets rose from the back of his neck and jerked into place forming a sort of helmet. When the surface of his body was completely covered, the metal started to shift and take on the appearance of armor. The face of the helmet resembled that of one the black carousel horse's face. Loner couldn't muster a snide comment. He drew on his cigarette again, then flicked it into the distance. He took off into Mateo's direction. Mateo continued a steady pace towards the girl. Loner flexed and drove off his rear foot as he cocked back his right fist. He pummeled through the air and unloaded his fist into Mateo. CRRRT-UNK-WUMP. The sheer force launched Loner backwards. Mateo slid inches backwards.

Concern filled Loner's face. He lunged again. Mateo lifted a heavy arm, soaking up the powerful punch, barely moving from the impact. Loner began to throw calculated combinations meeting similar results. The ends on Mateo's arms manipulated into large mace like orbs. He began to swing punches back slow and lethargic. WUMPHH. The sound of his heavy arms breezed by Loner's head. Loner continued to land successful punches one after another with no visible results, or advantage taken. GRRT. Loner started to back pedal. He needed a little more juice. Whatever just happened, Mateo was capable of taking every punch he could pack. Did he........... Did he absorb the carousel? He........ he was heavy...slow....dense. Mateo turned and started marching towards Fathom again. Loner lunged and landed a loaded punch. Little to no effect. Mateo continued his march. Loner stood and took a deep breath. "I really don't want to....," he said hesitantly as he reached into his back, left pocket. He looked down at the medical pen in his hand. He looked at Fathom, looked back at the pen. And then pressed it firmly against his thigh forcing its activation. He felt the epinephrine course through his body. His pulse quickened, and his chest got tight. "YEEERGGHHHH," he screamed. He took short breathes in and out to try and regulate. His eyes continued to dilate.

"HEH, HAH, HERAH," he gruffed. He forced a flex. GRRT. He pressed off his back foot and lunged at the back of his armor crusted brother.

Chapter Twelve: Fathom

Her eyes fluttered open. Her mind raced as she tried to contemplate where she was. She looked down at her hands to be met with her gloves and her uniform dusty. She lifted her head and witnessed the rubble surrounding her. Confusion continued to overcome her as she woke from her daze. Metallic sounds plinked in the distance. She rose to her feet and surveyed the area. She cupped her hands over her mouth as she saw black smoke spiraling up from the ground.

"Emmitt," she whimpered.

The metallic plinks continued, she pivoted her head to investigate. Her eyes continued to focus. There was a bulky figure engaging a smaller one. Incoherent noises were muttered between the two. She rubbed her eyes and tried to focus harder. She slowly regained her sight and realized the smaller figure was Loner. What was wrong with his eyes? She blinked hard a few more times. He looked enraged. Blood ran from his eyes and ears. He breathed heavily through clenched teeth. He looked almost feral. His hoodie was torn and tattered which exposed cuts and bruises riddling his body.

"LONER!" she called out.

The large mass he was engaging turned to investigate. Loner pounced and landed a heavy right hook to the back of its shoulder making it face plant into the ground immediately in front of it. Loner sprinted to it and clambered on top, unleashing a flurry of punches visibly denting the mass. Guttural growls and shouts emitted from Loner's mouth as he continued his assault. Large spikes erupted from the mass's back, launching Loner into the air.

"LONER!" Fathom shouted again.

The mass rose to its feet and continued to advance in her direction. Fear overtook her mind.

"RUN!" Loner choked out as he muttered in between his guttural noises.

Fathom froze in place and started to tremble. The past week's events ran through her mind. Losing Lingo. Seeing Ms. Greggers die. Losing Emmitt in the crash. Why? Why was this happening? Weren't we the good guys? Shouldn't we win? Why wasn't anyone helping?

"FATHOM!" Loner choked out again, "RUN!"

She continued to lose herself in pity and thought. There were so many people with powers. Abilities. And what do they do with them? Why won't they help? Why help tear apart this city? Why take children?

Loner lunged again and tackled the large metallic mass. He dug his fingers into the plating and tore portions off. He called out again, "FATHOM.....I...I CAN"T....KEEP THIS UP." He continued calculated and precise punches just to be thrown off again with projected spikes.

Who would protect us? I'm weak. I'm too young. I can't even help them. I just get in the way. Doubt continued to cloud her mind. As Loner hit the ground, he slid, and she heard a faint sound of stretching leather. Loner slumped to his side, clutching his ribs and howling in pain. He rolled to his stomach and used his face and head to push himself up to his knees. He was muttering something incoherent. And the mass of metal continued to make its way towards her.

"Loner?" she meekly called to him. He continued to writhe in pain. "Oh my god," she whimpered. He was dying she thought to herself. Everything else fell to the back of her mind. No one was coming. No one was going to come help. But he did. Loner came to protect them. Now he needed protecting. She had to be strong. Franchise called her a young hero. She needed to be. She took off in a run to Loner. As she approached, the club end of Mateo's arm split into tendrils and wrapped around her waist, lifting her into the air.

"GAAHHHH," she screamed. The tendrils retracted and placed Fathom in front of its face. His helmet retracted, and her wide eyes met the smug grin of Mateo.

"LET ME GO!" she screamed.

Her scream was met with short chuckles. "All of that?" Mateo started, "For this?"

His grin was met with a stern grimace on Fathom's face. She outstretched her hands and tried to focus. As pale blue spirals spun from her hands, Mateo tightened the coils around her. "GAAAHH," she belted as her energy dissipated. Slight chuckles were heard from behind the two. Mateo pivoted to look at an exhausted Loner clutching his ribs.

"Hey kiddo," Loner managed to muttered. "You know....this carnival.....you know what it reminds me of?" Loner said followed by struggling chuckles. Fathom looked over in despair. Mateo shot an annoyed looked at Fathom, then to Loner, then back at Fathom.

In disgusted curiosity, Mateo questioned, "What is that?"

Loner forced through a few more chuckles. "When I was a little kid," Loner coughed, "me and my little brother used to play with this one toy." Loner paused and ensured he had Fathoms eye contact. "It was a simple. Little. Toy. Robot."

His comments were met with a slight squint from Fathom. With that faint signal Loner broke into as much of a run as he could muster. Mateo turned to face Loner and unknowingly loosened his coils on Fathom. GRRT. Loner drove off the ground and cocked back a fist while whizzing through the air. Fathom threw open her hands and spirals of dull blue emitted from them. In front of Mateo, the image of the simple storage robot started to fabricate.

I need to help she thought to herself. Miles needed to help. We need to help Loner. Together…..we could win. Loner barreled through the air. As he began to pass through the new robot Miles, Fathom's eyes pour out a bright bluish light that radiated down her face.

Loner felt… pure joy and innocence wash away all the pain and ache from his head and body. As he connected his right hook, he realized the giant robotic pincer three feet away from the tip of his fist. He firmly planted his feet on the ground. Or so he thought. Mateo tumbled backwards, releasing Fathom in the process. Loner looked down to see his legs surrounded by the blocky legs of the robot Miles. Encased within the large toy robot, his actual feet hovered four feet above the ground. He turned to look at Fathom in disbelief, only to see the bright glow flow from her eyes.

Fathom looked at Loner, floating in the middle of Miles. Much like she was able to do by herself. But there was something different. She moved her arms, yet Miles didn't move. She tilted her head as she studied Loner's face. His eyes were glowing. A bright bluish light flowed from them. Loner looked at each hand and opened and closed each. In amazement, he watched the pincers open and close. GRRT, he unflexed and pivoted his hips to witness Miles imitate.

Loner felt calm and relaxed. All worry seemed to fade away. He looked up in admiration and spoke softly, "What is this?"

Fathom looked back in disbelief and said plainly, "I don't know."

Mateo charged in and attempted to tackle Loner, who was now surrounded and completely inside Miles. Loner looked over calmly and pivoted their block feet. As if moving a puppet, he manipulated the pincers, gripped and pushed back on Mateo. Mateo broke free of a pincer, then landed a hook with little impact. He thrust his palm under the chin of the robot and unleashed a fury of needles that impacted and crumpled instantly. Mateo flicked the same wrist. A metal pike, five feet in length, formed, attached to his palm. He pivoted his hips and attempted to thrust the pike into the midsection of Miles. The tip slid back and forth with the sheer force and pressure but does not puncture. Loner swung the massive claw repeatedly, knocking Mateo off balance. Mateo pounded his fists on the ground in frustration. Suddenly he directed his attention towards Fathom. He realized this blue figure must be a product of her. He pushed forward and shoved off Loner to gain momentum. As he drew closer to Fathom, metallic tendrils erupted from his back and shoulders. As they curved, they tunneled through the air to grasp at her again. GRRT. Loner spun his claws and threw an over hand right, colliding with Mateo, pinning him to the ground. Although Mateo stopped forward momentum, his tendrils continued towards Fathom. Loner clenched his fist, consequently smashing the pincer closed around Mateo. He pushed into his pincer and ripped backward over his head, slamming him into the ground behind him. Loner continued this process forward and backwards several times before releasing his grasp, letting a limp Mateo fell to the ground. GRRT. As Loner released his flex, he felt the calm and peace leave from his head. He fell to the ground, the pain seared through his body once again. He clutched at his ribs and eyes. He peered through squinted eyes to see Fathom hit both her knees. Puzzled, he struggled to open his eyes. Fathom fell forward onto her face. Two dart-like objects protruded from the back of her shoulder. Loner's eyes darted upwards in disbelief to an unwelcome familiar face.

"Hope the kid wakes up. Those trancs were designed for you," stated the man Loner only knew as Captain Dickbag.

Hopper:

Hopper continued to cover his mouth as he kicked in a nearby mirror. THWIP. One of Franchise's bolts crashed through another. Through the dense smoke, reflections of Mirrors holding a choking Gracie shimmer.

"Gawd dang fun house," Hopper coughed.

"KEEP," Franchise choked out, "BREAKING THE MIRRORS!"

"IMMA BREAK THE WALL DOWN," Hopper sputtered.

"NO," Franchise spat back, "RISK. HURTING. GRACIE."

The smoke was intense. Once again, Hopper stood in an enclosed space, dowsed in dense smoke. His eyes burned as he squinted through. Another flash in the mirror. Hopper sent out another kick, shattering the mirror. THWIP, another of Franchise's bolts shattered another. Hopper squinted his eyes harder, trying to focus through the fog. He tried to map out his surroundings by putting his hands up in front of him waving them around. He pressed against a wall coughing and sputtering, walking himself down the length of it. Finally, he found the corner. He couldn't breathe anymore. He couldn't see anymore. He wanted out. He disregarded Franchise as he reared back a leg and landed a powerful kick towards the corner. The contained smoke scurried out the opening and light shined in. Hopper peered his head out and breathed in deeply. He turned around and stepped to the side to allow the light to illuminate the crowded fun house. He could finally see the outline of the course.

"YOU COULD'VE HURT GRACIE," Franchise shouted.

"AND YA CROSSBOW AIN'T?" Hopper shot back. "Look mayne…they ain't in here no more." He turned and kicked through a bigger portion of the wall. He stepped through and looked about. "We need your eyes mayne."

Franchise hurried through the opening and started to analyze. Nothing. He locked eyes with Hopper and muttered, "Get airborne." With a simple nod, they thrust into the air. Franchise hovered in the air, rotating slowly, scanning the area. He grimaced as he found fifteen large vans parked in a herringbone formation near the middle of fairground. About twenty people in a group surrounding one person hunched over. That must be Loner. He continued to analyze. FATHOM! She was unconscious on the ground in front of Loner. He barreled through the air towards her.

"WHAT? YOU FIND HER?" Hopper shouted as he descended to the ground. He hit the ground and started to run in his direction keeping his eyes locked on Franchise. As Franchise descended, Hopper finally saw the group of armed men. "Aw, mayne," he muttered to himself.

Franchise and Hopper jogged up to Loner's side with concerned looks on their faces. Hopper looked down at Fathom and

Mateo splayed on the ground. He jutted forward to grab Fathom but was stopped by Loner gripping his arm. In the same instant, every man, except one, raised their weapon to their shoulder. Ready to fire.

"Uh…Loner?" Hopper said in a low tone.

Loner, still hunched over, continued to lock eyes with the man in front. Four of the men in the group gathered around Mateo, and they struggled to drag him to one of the vans. The back opened, and four more men piled out. The eight of them struggled as they lifted Mateo and slumped him into the back. The van visibly sank towards the ground from the weight. With Mateo in the back, the van spun its tires and fell in line with two others. As it turned, Franchise saw the piercing eyes and gnarled grin of Smoke as he reached forward and closed the door to the van.

"THEY HAVE GRACIE!" Franchise screamed as he attempted to launch into the air. Loner grabbed material on his suit and planted him on the ground. He then fixed his stare back on the man in the front. "Loner, please!" Franchise pleaded, "They have her!"

"They also have guns. Lots," Loner grumbled and wheezed. "You wouldn't get far. You're not bulletproof." Franchise fell into a panic, looking left and right.

"Find something mayne," Hopper whispered. Frantically, Franchise started to analyze as he fell into the back of his mind. Twenty men. Each with rifles and body armor. Twelve armored vehicles. Armored vehicles. "Loner….I'm not bullet proof….but their vans are," he said in a low tone.

Loner closed his eyes and drew in a deep breath. He pried open his eyes and darted them left and right. The front vehicle on his left was closest. If he moved, they'd shoot.

"The moment one of us moves, they're going to open up a shooting gallery. I can't move the van……but Hopper can," Loner said plainly.

"Wait. What?" Hopper started. GRRT. Loner pushed outwards sending the other two heroes sideways. He leaned forward and launched himself into a flurry of gunshots. Barrel flashes burned his eyes. He felt his clothes tatter and fray as bullets struck his skin. He landed a heavy right hand down onto Captain Dickbag's chin, down into his collarbone. The captain muttered and gargled on blood. The shots fired lessened. Loner didn't have much left in the tank. Nineteen to one still weren't good odds. He made a decision. As Captain Dickbag continued to sputter and gag on teeth and blood, Loner leaned down, grabbed under the captain's armpit and hip, and raised him above his head. The bullets stopped. Loner let his arms drop in front of his face and then ripped both his arms backwards, letting out a guttural scream. The innards of their previous captain splattered the gunmen. Fear, Loner thought to himself. This was how they win this one. He launched forward with either half of the late captain still in his hands. Loner landed another downwards right into one of the gunmen, crumpling him to the ground. The other gunmen turned and scrambled to their vehicles. Loner dropped the two halves and approached the van on the left. He forcefully pulled a tire off and launched it at another gunman, knocking him to the ground. The others climbed into several vehicles and peeled off into the streets, leaving three vehicles. GRRT. Loner slumped to the ground and covered his eyes. Hot sticky blood saturated his face.

Hopper stood there speechless. He landed and watched the entire thing. Grotesque. Brutal. He shuttered at the carnage. All the commotion going on around, Hopper didn't hear a thing. Numbness fell over him. In his peripheral, he saw Franchise tending to Fathom. Hopper started to realize the noises around him. Loner was panting something. Hopper turned to acknowledge.

"Hey…..hey….that one guy…..the tire….he's still alive," Loner panted out.

"What? Do I need to……?" Hopper started.

"Information kid….." Loner offered. "Access to SYNERGY. He…..might know…..or its… in the vans…"

"You…..you…tore a man in half…." Hopper mumbled.

"You're welcome," Loner chuckled as he picked a flattened bullet out of his shoulder.

Franchise dragged Fathom over to Hopper and placed her at his feet. Then he stormed over to the gunman's side. "AAAAHHH ….my…my back!" the gunman screamed.

"WHERE DID THEY TAKE THEM?" Franchise yelled.

"AHH, AHH, it's just a job man. Just…just a security job," the gunman chattered.

"Where. Did they take them?" Franchise stated again sternly.

"Don't kill me! I…I have a family…." The gunman pleaded.

Franchise positioned his face next to the gunman's and said coldly, "Where?"

"B-b-b-ack to SYNERGY," he muttered.

"How do we get in there?" Franchise continued to interrogate.

"Y-y-y-ou can't. They let you in."

"What are they going to do with the girl?" Franchise asked aggressively.

"I-I-I don't know. I was just supposed to pick up and drop off. I swear!"

Sirens blazed in the background and surged closer. Lights flickered in the background and illuminated high off the windows of buildings. Loner peered through his bloody eyes, "We gotta go before it gets real interesting kids." Franchise stood and looked backwards. Hopper seized with fear. Fathom unconscious. Loner in shambles. Emmitt lost. Gracie taken. His heart sunk. "What have I done?" he whimpered.

Loner pushed, "One of those vans......probably has keys in it. We....gotta go..."

"Where? We can't go back to base. We can't....go to SYNERGY.... like this," Franchise said pathetically.

Loner chuckled through the moaning of the gunman, "If we stay, we go to jail. We need to get Barnaby and my stuff. Then ya'll can...figure the rest out. I've done my part." Stricken with the reality, Franchise walked to the vans. The sirens grew closer. Franchise turned the keys in the ignition and fired up the van. He and Hopper gently placed Fathom into the back. The two dragged Loner to the back as Hopper asked, "What about him?" hinting towards the gunman.

"Ambulances have sirens," Loner coughed out as the two loaded him into the back. Franchise removed his goggles and got into the driver's seat. He pressed down the gas and headed towards the warehouse. The cab was solemn between Franchise and Hopper. Hopper looked through the grating into the back at a crumbled Fathom and Loner.

"It wasn't supposed to be like this mayne," Hopper started sulking.

"I know," Franchise stated.

"You said we were going to help people," Hopper continued.

"We are--"

"WE JUST KILLED A GUY!" Hopper shouted, "And left another in the fricken street to die? How? How are you ok with this?"

Franchise started to shudder, and tears started to run down his face. The realization overcame him all at once. They were over their heads. If Loner wasn't there... they would have lost everyone. Or worse. They weren't enough. They weren't strong. They weren't smart. Chasing a pipe dream.

They pulled into the driveway of the warehouse. "Barnaby knows…what I need," Loner muttered. Hopper and Franchise exited the van and entered the warehouse. Franchise stomped past Barnaby reading a magazine in the living areas. Hopper engaged a startled Barnaby about Loner's 'stuff'. He clambered around and picked up a back pack and Loner's satchel. Franchise continued down the hallway. He opened a large bag and started scooping parts, tools and, equipment into it. Scraps of notes, blueprints, and newly designed bolts for his crossbow. He dragged it behind him down the hall following Barnaby and Hopper back to the van. They helped Barnaby into the back with the bag of parts.

"Oh, my…" Barnaby chirped in surprise.

"Trying a new looked," Loner chuckled in short breaths.

Franchise slammed the driver's door shut and asked, "Where to next?"

Loner coughed and moaned, "Food. Water. Medical supplies for a few days. Barnaby looks normal enough for shopping."

"Then what?" Hopper snapped.

"I don't fucking know man. Hide under a bridge until you figure out what's next?"

Before the injured Loner and Hopper could continue their argument, a distant Franchise interrupted, "Where's the nearest store? Away from the police." The group looked around at each other. Barnaby fumbled around in the back for a minute. "Here's a map," he offered as he rolled it up and stuck it between the grates. Franchise retrieved it and opened it up. The SYNERGY logo was branded in the top right corner.

His eyes widened, "This isn't a map." Hopper and Barnaby looked over in curiosity. "It's the layout of SYNERGY. Well, at least the loading dock and base floor."

Hopper reluctantly asked, "What does that mean?"

"It means we're going to get Lingo and Gracie back," Franchise stated, studying the plans. He folded them and started the van. "Food, water, and supplies. Hide under a bridge for a few days. Then to SYNERGY." His words resounded with Hopper. Hopper gave a reluctant nod and looked back at the incapacitated Fathom and feeble Loner.

"You really think we can?" he prodded.

"We have to," Franchise offered. "For Lingo. For Gracie….."

"My brother….." Loner grumbled.

"We have to…," Franchise repeated.

A small camera in the dash whirled and focused on the team, undiscovered.

The Engineer:

The heroes appeared on the Engineer's display through the camera. "They have one of our vehicles," the Engineer stated plainly.

"So, they do," Boss Winston acknowledged.

"And what happens if they come here?" Dr. Monroe quipped.

"We let them in," Boss Winston said with a smirk.

"Let them in?" Dr. Monroe asked puzzled.

"This facility is impenetrable," the Engineer stated.

"I know it is, Engineer," Boss Winston said, patting him on the shoulder. "That's why we'll have to let them in.'"

"To do what exactly?" Dr. Monroe questioned.

"We want the girl. They'll bring her to us.," Boss Winston said through his existing smirk.

"Damage to the facility is unavoidable," the Engineer stated.

"Nothing, a little TLC, won't fix," Boss Winston chuckled.

"What of the other subjects? The girl and Loner are unpredictable. Are you really willing to risk all of our progress?" pleaded Dr. Monroe.

"Oh yes," Boss Winston replied. "Plus, this would be a good time to test your newest subject. Wouldn't you say? I'm eager to see if it's worth the investment."

"The Greggers boy?" Dr. Monroe pried.

"Yes. That one. Make sure it's ready to meet our visitors Dr. Monroe. And Engineer, ensure the Balcony is ready to receive visitors. This should be entertaining to watch."

Chapter Thirteen: Heroes for the People

Barnaby huffed and puffed behind the steering wheel, almost hyperventilating. It had been five days since the fair grounds. The events were all over the news. Fathom had awoken, and Loner had regained most of his strength. The team was hesitant of what laid in front of them. Their confiscated van sat alongside the wood line, bordering the chain link fence that surrounded the elusive SYNERGY Corporation. Fathom sat nervously rocking back and forth with her hands on her knees. Franchise put his hand on her shoulder, "We're going to get them back." She gave a few nervous nods. Loner sat against the door sewing his 'L' emblem onto a new sweatshirt. Hopper sat with his elbows on his knees and palms pressed against his face.

"Everyone have their gear?" Franchise asked.

"Yeah," responded Hopper. Fathom continued to nod. Loner gripped the last pair of glasses on his head and slipped them over his eyes.

"Ok, we're going to go through the back-supply dock," Franchise started.

"Last time I went in there, there were a lot of guys. Everywhere. Some with forklift suits," Loner interrupted.

"So, we'll distract and move past," Franchise continued. "You two," he pointed at Hopper and Loner, "can move equipment or obstacles to mask our movement and let us gain access to the rear hallway."

"This is crazy mayne," Hopper chimed in. "We don't even know where they are keeping them. So, we just going to wander around?"

"I've memorized the map Hopper. I can navigate this floor," Franchise reassured.

Hopper pointed at the building, "There's more than one floor!"

"If they aren't there, then I'll figure it out," Franchise said calmly.

"This is crazy!" Hopper said defeated.

Franchise continued, "Mr. Barnaby…you'll stay in the woods, and pick us up when we get outside." Barnaby rapidly nodded. Loner finished his last stitch and bit off the extra string. He placed his hand on the knob of the back door and pushed it open.

"Wait, Loner! I'm not….," Franchise panicked.

Loner stepped out and started walking towards the building, "Sounds like there is no plan. Open the door, look for the girls. Got it." He rolled his shoulders as he walked to the building, warming up.

"This ain't right," Hopper said, as he stepped out of the van.

"Come young hero," Franchise said to Fathom with a smile, "It's time to rescue Lingo and Gracie."

Fathom forced a smile and followed close behind Franchise. They approached the rolling back door of SYNERGY. Loner squatted down and gripped under the door.

He looked over his shoulder as he warned, "I'd stay back if I were ya'll."

GRRT. He jerked up, and military pressed a portion of the gate up. He stepped in with his fists up, ready. He looked around quickly left and right. The receiving dock was empty. He grunted and walked fully inside. Boxes and crates were scattered everywhere much like before. But there were no workers, no soldiers, no robot suits. He turned to call over his shoulder, "HEY." But the three have followed him in already. Loner looked at Franchise, furrowed his brow and shook his head 'no.'

"We keep going," Franchise announced. They wandered into the middle of the floor when they all heard mechanical movement. Loud ticking and gears grinding resonated throughout the room.

"I fricken told ya so!" Hopper snapped.

Large, four-inch-thick barriers quickly lowered behind them, covering the gate they just came through. CRKTCRKTCRKT. CRKTCRKTCRKT. Loner jogged to it as it lowered to chest height. He grasped under it with his hands and pushed up in his flex. The panel continued to lower methodically. Loner groaned as he lost ground. Against Loner's strength, the wall continued to inch towards the ground. Loner released the door as it slammed to the ground. He peered around to see panels slam down barring off several other doors. The others looked at him hopelessly. He offered a slight shrug. The lights dimmed. Lights flickered three times in the one doorway that was unbarred. The group looked at each other. The light flickered three times again. Hopper shook his head left to right.

Franchise looked around, "It's the only way." He took off walking in that direction, with Fathom following close behind.

Loner cracked his neck and followed, with Hopper right after. A long white hallway awaited them. The light continued to flicker. They came upon another metal gate that had been lowered.

"Now what?" Hopper shouted.

The door slid open. SHINK. They walked through into a hallway that stretched left and right. A simple sign was hanging on the wall in front of them. 'Laboratory' with an arrow to the left, and 'Workshop' with an arrow to the right.

"Laboratory is bad news," Loner started, "Gorge and Meat came out of that place."

"Looks like we're going to the workshop," said Franchise.

The group took a right and walked down another barren flickering hallway. As they proceeded, they heard the sounds of metal grinding and electricity flowing. At the end of the hallway, another metallic door shifted open. SHINK. The group pressed forward into a dim room lit with neon lights and filled with monitors and electronics. It was hard to see. Neon lights flickered and illuminated benches with mechanical parts strewn throughout them.

"Oww," Fathom remarked as she bumped her face into something.

She put her hands up and felt around on a wall. Franchise ran his hands on the same wall. After further inspection, it revealed to be inches thick of see through plastic.

"See if you can break through," Franchise told Loner. Loner gave a quick nod, flexed and unloaded a punch into it. The wall shook with a resounding thud.

"What now?" questioned Hopper. Franchise shook his head with concern.

Footsteps could be heard coming from the rear of the workshop. The metallic clack of steel toed boots. The group anticipated the worst. Out of the shadows a thin, short statured man, with a shaved head walked into view. He wore blue jeans and a white tank top littered with black splotches. His eyes flew up to the group standing behind the saw-through wall. His facial expression didn't change. He continued his methodical walk over to a large console filled of keys, switches, and monitors. As he turned, light glinted off of his purple and magenta gauntlet on his left hand. He sat at the console and his hands flew across the assembly, clicking keys and switches.

"The Engineer?" Loner said aloud. The group shook their heads puzzled.

"Benjamin," the Engineer called, "run diagnostics on the organic translator project."

"Yes father," the console responded to him.

A few feet from the console, a mechanized container whirled, and steam hissed out of it as gears and pistons moved. The large egg-shaped container's panels splayed open and emitted a bright whitish blue light. The Heroes winced and protected their eyes with their arms. As Franchise lowered his arms from his face, his stomach turned, and he couldn't breathe.

"Aw, no mayne," Hopper gasped.

Fathom covered her mouth with her hands and whimpered, "That's Lingo."

Through coils and wires, you could see the semblance of a human figure. Now mostly machine, you could still distinguish where her neck would be. Wires and cords plugged into her jawline, with what appeared to be a voice speaker assembled where her lips used to be. Her eyes had been replaced with contoured hexagon screens with binary codes rapidly flashing across them. A metallic hood covered her forehead and her ears towards the back of her head.

"What have they done?" Franchise choked out.

"Systems at 73%. Download and integration near complete," the computer stated.

"Thank you, Benjamin," the Engineer said looking at the computer screens. "Have this system start to decrypt the cosmic dialogue."

"Yes father," the computer responded.

"Cosmic?" Loner repeated lowly.

"WHY?" Franchise cried, "WHY DID YOU DO THIS?"

The Engineer turned in his chair and slowly stood. He said coldly, "You four are expected at the Balcony." He turned a dial on his gauntlet and pressed a button. Instantly, the door shut behind them and another to their left opened.

"WE'RE NOT GOING ANYWHERE," Franchise screamed, "GET HER OUT OF THERE. GET…GET HER…out."

"I suggest you get moving," the Engineer said plainly through steely eyes.

Franchise fell to his knees whimpering and crying, "Lingo, I didn't mean. Not like this….I'm so sorry."

"Benjamin, prepare my armor," the Engineer called to the computer again.

"Yes, father." Across the room, another door slid open. A hulking mass of bluish grey armor stepped out. Cables hissed as they disconnected and retracted into the room it came from. The suit of armor glinted in the neon light. Perfectly symmetric, ending with what looked like a medieval knight's helmet. Complete with a long red tassel flowing from the crown of the helmet. The shoulders housed large turbines on either side that seemed to turn slowly. The Engineer walked to it and placed his back towards it, toggling with his gauntlet again. The chest and legs flayed open to reveal padding and several small consoles inside. He stepped back into it, sliding his legs and arms into place. He manipulated his fingers through the suit, then the panels collapsed, closing the suit around him. With large, piston sounding steps, he approached the glass.

///MOVE TO THE BALCONY/// the Engineer beckoned through the suit.

Loner tensed up as he peered over to see his fear stricken group. Franchise continued his frantic grieving and crumbled to the ground.

///PERHAPS YOU NEED ASSISTANCE/// the Engineer beckoned again. He tilted the arm of the suit, and a panel slid backwards. He pressed several buttons on the exposed control pad. A loud CLUNK was heard as a portion of the ceiling slid open to their right down the hallway. SHINK. TURTUNK. Two solid metal feet hit the ground. The metallic figure braced its impact, then rose to a standing position. Rapid wind movement echoed through the hallway. Loner recognized Terror-cane immediately.

"Time to go!" Loner exclaimed as he grabbed the scruff of Franchise's suit and Fathom's arm.

"Another robot?" Hopper asked confused. The core of Terror-cane pulsed as the torrent whipped inside.

"You don't understand kiddo. We gotta…," Loner started.

Terror-cane placed the cores of its arms pointing towards the corners of the walls. They erupted with a tremendous burst of wind. The two gusts hit and spun down the hallway. The group was spun into the air, propelled down the hallway, hitting the walls and ceiling on the way down. Loner clambered to his feet and quickly picked up the other members.

"LET'S GO!" he screamed.

The team ran through the halls, taking the turns that they were allowed. Dark. Hard to see. Flickering lights. Luckily no Terror-cane behind them. A bright light up ahead. Loner, in front, slowed his pace. He heard another whir behind him. He cautioned and lead the members forward.

He put his arm up to block the bright light as he squinted his eyes. His eyes began to focus again as he heard a CLUNK behind him. He turned to see another metal barrier close and lock them in. He slowly turned to take in his new environment. They were in a large dome like room. Various doors along the walls. He looked up again trying to shade his eyes from the bright light. There seemed to be a platform. With two people standing on top of it, watching over the dome. The group inched forward to discover more of their surroundings.

A thick drawl came over an intercom into the dome, "Welcome."

"Who is this?" demanded Franchise, "What have you done to Lingo? Where is Gracie?"

"Me?" the voice answered, "Around here, people address me as Winston."

A piercing feeling ran through Loner's spine. "Where is Mateo?" he called out into the Balcony.

"Recovering," Boss Winston said in a solemn tone, "you really did a number on that poor child."

"LINGO! GRACIE!" Franchise screamed, "WHAT HAVE YOU DONE!"

"Preparation," Boss Winston answered.

"What?" Fathom meekly asked.

"Preparation for what?" Franchise cried.

"Something. Everything. Or nothing," Boss Winston chuckled. "Something is coming son. People. Things. War. Something will happen. And the person with the most weapons," he paused, "normally wins."

"Your building weapons?" asked Hopper, "Then what did you do to Lingo?"

"McCray?" Boss Winston assured, "A very useful tool."

"And Gracie?" chimed Fathom.

"Will be a very useful tool. Much more dangerous to tamper with than a mere translator."

Franchise yelled as he swung his left arm up, engaging his crossbow and firing off a bolt. It collided with the barrier around the balcony, shattering the bolt, leaving the barrier unscratched.

"Lingo was a good person, who just wanted purpose. And Gracie is just a child!" Franchise cried out.

"Oh, I agree son. McCray now has a very important purpose. And so will the young lady," Boss Winston answered.

Loner paid attention to the words he was saying. How he was saying them. His drawl and the way he continued to use son in his speech. Loner thought to himself that Mateo was taken so young, that over time....he must've thought he was being called his actual son. Loner realized that the longer Boss Winston talked, the more information he could gather. "Why the girl?" Loner pried.

"Mind control is a very powerful thing," Boss Winston continued, "something I don't want to be on the receiving end of."

"How do you plan to use it? Her?" Loner questioned.

"Some of our experiments...don't seem to have much direction. As powerful weapons as they could be, they don't listen very well," Boss Winston said with a smile.

"Meat...," Loner said shortly.

"Smart boy," Boss Winston replied.

"Why me?" Franchise muttered, "Why my list?"

"Well, you made it easy son," Boss Winston said with a laugh, "You pulled them off public internet." Franchise's heart sunk. Boss Winston continued, "Some we already had a bead on. But some, like Ms. McCray. Well, she was a good find."

"This is my fault," Franchise muttered, "all my fault." Franchise looked feet in front of him with a distant look in his eyes.

"Why her?" Loner said pointing at Fathom.

"Me?" Fathom yelped.

"Yes, you darlin," Boss Winston said almost with compassion in his voice. "You are something special. Anything you can think of. Poof. There it is. Amazing."

"You'd use the FULCRUM on her?" Loner queried.

"Oh lord no," Boss Winston said with a chuckle. This was met with a grunt by the nearby Dr. Monroe who stood next to him with his arms crossed. Boss Winston continued, "With a gift that delicate, I wouldn't dare."

"Then on Gracie?" Loner asked.

"No son, not on something that can be nurtured," Boss Winston stated.

"So, what's next Winston?" Loner decided to cut to the chase.

"Well, you already brought me the girl, Loner. Just like you were supposed to," Boss Winston said with a smile. Hopper, Franchise, and Fathom slowly turned their heads to glance at Loner. "Cut it out," Loner snapped. "And what if we say no?"

The Engineer in his armor stepped onto the Balcony from the other side. As he walked up, Boss Winston gave him a nod. The panel on his left arm slid open again as he pressed a few buttons. Two doors slid upwards, revealing Meat and Gorge behind multiple bars. Heavy groaning and breathing come from Meats' cell.

A guttural growl bellowed from Gorge, then followed by sniffing of the air. "IIIIIS SMEEEELLLLLSSSS YOOOOUUUU," Gorge growled as he lifted a gargantuan disfigured hand at Loner.

Gorge was now roughly six and a half, or seven feet tall. Probably four or five hundred pounds. He had the figure of a bloated disfigured man. His mouth ran from his nose down his throat and ended on top of his chest. Gnarled teeth scattered throughout. Heavy dark circles shaded his nearly blacked out eyes. His flabby, bloated gut hung over shreds of pants it still wore. Fathom started to back up and Franchise rose to his feet in awe.

Loner was hesitant to ask the following question. "What did Gorge....eat?"

"Failed experiments," Dr. Monroe quipped, "and a few reluctant handlers."

"What are they for?" Loner pressed.

///FAILSAFE IF THE DOCTORS NEW ABOMINATION FAILS/// the Engineer jeered. This was met with another disgruntled grunt from Dr. Monroe.

"Gentlemen," Boss Winston started, "there is a civil way to end this. I wouldn't dare to lose an opportunity to gain useful, talented employees."

"Work? For you?" Franchise asked if he had heard something wrong.

"That's right my boy. We all get what we want. You can continue to play hero and find other talented individuals. And I continue to prepare for whatever comes next," Boss Winston suggested.

"After what you did to Lingo? Emmitt? Ms. Greggers? Our Home? And now you want us....to help you?" Franchise shot back.

"Bygones and all," replied Boss Winston.

"Never," sneered Franchise.

"And does he speak for you all?" Boss Winston asked with an outstretched hand gesturing to the group. They all remained silent. "So be it," Boss Winston said as he gave a nod to the Engineer. The Engineer pressed two buttons on his arm, and a circle in the middle of the room splayed open. A glass container rose slowly. Buzzing, clicking, and chattering resonating from within accompanied with shrieks and shrill cries. What seemed to be a cloud, ricocheted off the sides on the container on the inside. After it collided with a side, the cloud consolidated into a shape that resembled a human boy. "EEEEIIIIIAAAAAHHHHH," a scream emitted from the container.

"Let me introduce experiment 2876," said Dr. Monroe in an accomplished tone.

"MY SKIN. IT'S, IT'S CRAWLING. AAHH, I CAN'T. MY EYES!" screamed the experiment. From its boy shape, it burst back into a cloud and ricocheted off the glass again, like insects trying to head to the light.

"Are those....bugs?" Fathom shrieked.

"Oh yes girl," Dr. Monroe said proudly, "another experiment on adaption. Able to use pheromones to attract any native species and apply them to its mass. Able to adapt to nearly any environment."

"Pheromones?" Franchise said in disbelief, "Is that.....is that ....Ripley?"

"Was," said Dr. Monroe smugly. "But with the aid of FULCRUM," he said looking at Boss Winston out of the side of his eyes, "he's better now."

"SSHHREEEEEEEIIIAAHHHH," echoed from the container, "MY HEAD. IT'S SO LOUD. IT. WON'T STOP."

"BUG," announced Boss Winston, "the dear doctor may be able to reverse this process." This message was met with more shrieks and clicks. "If only you would eliminate the men in your cage. Leave the girl alive, and I promise the dear doctor will try his hardest to find a cure." More shrieks and clicking echoed from the container. "Do we have a deal, BUG?" The cloud of insects consolidated into the shape of a boy once again.

The buzzing and clicking mellowed until in a shrill voice, it answered, "RELEASE ME."

Boss Winston gave a nod to the Engineer. And with a press of a button, the top of the container shot upward, and the canister sunk back into the floor. In an instant, the figure burst back into a mass of chittering insects and swarmed the group. In a panic, Fathom, Franchise, and Hopper take off in different directions. GRRT. Loner loaded a right hand, and as BUG approached, he unloaded. The swarm split, and bit, scratched and stung him as it whizzed around his fist and arm. Loner turned in disbelief to see the swarm chase after Hopper. Loner looked down as he started to swat ants, flies, bees, and centipedes off his jacket. Hopper turned to see the swarm chase him down.

He pivoted in place and screamed, "Only room for one bug in here!"

He dug in his toes and leapt into the air. The swarm changed directions and followed him closely. Hopper swung a powerful kick with similar results as before. The swarm split and attacked his body with a flurry of bites and stings.

"AHHHHH," Hopper screamed in agony as he descended.

As he hit the ground, the swarm completely engulfed him. Just a chittering mass writhing and wriggling on top of his wailing and screams.

"HOPPER!" exclaimed Franchise.

He took aim with his crossbow, loaded a bolt, and fired. It hit the wriggling mass and exploded in tendrils of electricity. BUG shrieked and chittered as the swarm shot upwards and away from Hopper, letting the bolt fall to the ground. Exhausted, Hopper pushed himself to his knees. He breathed heavy as he revealed his heavily stung face. The swarm turned and pursued Franchise. He loaded another bolt and fell into analyzing. The entire swarm glowed. Every piece. Every insect.

"There's no queen!" he exclaimed.

Dr. Monroe chuckled, "No need for a queen. The former Ripley is the queen thanks to his pheromones."

The swarm hit Franchise and knocked him off his feet. As he hit the ground, the next bolt exploded into tendrils. BUG disconnected from Franchise and flew into the air. Franchise pushed himself up and methodically loaded another bolt.

"Seen enough?" Doctor Monroe asked Boss Winston with a cocked eyebrow.

"There's more?" questioned Boss Winston.

Doctor Monroe took a small test tube out of his lab coat. Under the cork, a praying mantis was constantly wrapping at the glass tube. Dr. Monroe used his thumb to pop the cork from the tube. The mantis quickly climbed out and fluttered to the floor, squeezing its way through the bottom of the Balcony. It hurried into the massive swarm that started to spiral around it. The swarm condensed into the form of a boy once again. Insects spiraled around its left arm mimicking the appearance of the mantis' scythe.

"Impressive dear doctor," praised Boss Winston.

"Remarkable," Dr. Monroe said in awe as he pressed his hands against the glass.

BUG swooped down at Loner and swung its massive scythe. Loner pivoted, letting the scythe impact the ground. GRRT. Loner landed a powerful punch into BUG. It exploded into different directions, then towards the ground. Loner looked down to see the mass spiraling up his leg from where the scythe impacted. As he reared back a fist, another bolt hit and erupted into tendrils of electricity sending BUG airborne again. GRRT. Loner unflexed. He looked up to see where it was going next. Hopper and Franchise both have their backs towards the edges of the dome, waiting. Loner started to back pedal. BUG reformed to human shape and reassemble its scythe. With a screech, it tore off in Hopper's direction. Feet away from a crouched Hopper, pale blue encompassed Bug. The orb guided towards the ground as feet, arms, and tassels of ear flowed out of it. Loner looked over to see Fathom in a firm stance with her hands outstretched, her hands glowing the same dull blue. He shifted his head to see BUG trapped inside of Miles, ricocheting around much like the container before.

"YES!" exclaimed Hopper, "So fricken happy to see Miles right now!"

"Valiant effort Doctor. Quite impressive," Boss Winston said as he turned to the Engineer, "release the others." Another click of a button and the bars containing Meat and Gorge slid down.

Loners eyes flew up. "GOD. FUCKING. DAMN IT," he yelled. Meat sluggishly stepped out into the surrounding dome. Gorge gurgled and quickly paced out of his cage. He let out a guttural growl. Loner knew the others won't be able to handle Gorge. He didn't know how long Fathom could restrain BUG. He breathed in deeply as he picked up a jog towards Gorge.

"PROTECT FATHOM!" he yelled over his shoulder, "WE NEED TO KEEP BUG WHERE HE IS!"

GRRT. He pushed off his back foot and launched at Gorge. Gorge's head tilted, and he fixed his eyes on Loner. As Loner soared through the air, Gorge trotted to the side and collided one stumpy hand along Loner's back, smacking him to the ground. Loner quickly turned onto his back to see the gaping mouth of Gorge snap and crack. Gorge's catcher mitt sized hands pawed at Loner, trying to grasp him and pull him into his mouth. Loner gripped the inside of Gorge's palms and pushed back as Gorge jerked forward and snapped his jaws.

"THIS TIMESSSS. IIISSSS EAATTSSS. IIISSS EEAATTSSS YYOOUUUU," Gorge growled.

He's more agile, Loner thought as he struggled back. His vision was better. But he's not as strong. Loner worked his knees to his chest as he struggled under Gorge's weight. He pushed hard and created distance between him and Gorge. As Gorge lunged back in to grasp at Loner, Loner rocked up on his shoulders and mule kicked Gorge in the chest with both legs, sending him tumbling backwards. Loner rolled to his side and looked quickly at the others.

Fathom continued to struggle as she held her hands, focused on keeping BUG inside Miles. Franchise was airborne, leading Meat away from Fathom, distracting it as Hopper swooped in with a powerful kick, then backed off once again. After each hit, Meat returned to following Franchise bobbing through the air. Perfect.

Loner turned his head to find Gorge scuttling towards him again with a howl. Loner pressed himself up to his feet. Just have to wear him out again. Use up his energy. Make him regress. Loner dug in his feet. Gorge wildly swung an overhead swipe downwards at Loner. Loner stepped to the side and caught his wrist as it came past his beltline. Loner dug his fingers into the skin and flesh of Gorge's arm. Gorge let out another howl. Loner jerked forward towards his hip keeping Gorge off balance as he unloaded left hooks into Gorge's shoulder. Gorge whipped his head over, trying to bite at Loner over his own shoulder. Over the slapping and smacking of Gorge's jaws, Loner heard the sound of bone grinding on bone. Between punches, he peered over at the others. After Hopper landed kick after kick on

Meat's skinless hide, segments of bone shifted out of its skin and encased the area. Nearly all its back was now covered in plates of bone.

"The fuck?" Loner muttered.

Gorge landed a sloppy punch to Loner's face as he was distracted. Loner released his grip as he spun. Gorge clambered to him, wildly swinging his hands trying to grab at Loner. Loner found his bearing and kicked backwards, gaining distance between him and the gothic horror.

Fathom dropped to a knee. She was exhausted. She quaked as she tried to hold her hands up. BUG violently ricocheted around inside of Miles, making him visibly move.

Loner called out to Franchise, "TAZE THE UGLY FUCKER. KEEP HIM DOWN. I HAVE AN IDEA."

Franchise nodded with a worried looked on his face. As Gorge approached, Franchise loaded a bolt and discharged it, smacking Gorge in the leg. Tendrils erupted, and Gorge howled in pain.

"HOPPER!" Loner called, "I NEED AN ASSIST."

Loner ran up behind Meat, jumped and landed a mighty blow to the back of its knee. Meat fell forward, catching itself with its hands, letting out a bellow. As it pushed up, Loner grasped at the boney plates on its back and began to jerk Meat backwards keeping it off balance.

"HOPPER, OVER FATHOM. THE ASSIST," Loner called.

Hopper ran over to Fathom with a puzzled looked on his face. Loner planted his back foot and jerked as hard as he could to his left. As Meat's mass shifted to the left, Loner planted his heels together and leaned backwards. He used the momentum to complete a few small spirals until Meat's feet and hands were off the ground. Loner continued to jerk and pick up momentum.

"HOPPER!" Loner growled through gritted teeth, "READY?"

"READY FOR WHAT MAYNE?!" Hopper shouted.

Loner completed one last spiral and launched Meat into the air, soaring into Hopper and Fathom's direction. "AIRBORNE NOW! AT MILES!" Loner screamed.

Hopper's eyes grew large as Meat bounded towards them. He pushed off and barreled upwards. As Meat came inches by him, Hopper loaded and released a powerful kick directed towards Miles.

"FATHOM! LET GO!" Loner screamed.

She let her hands fall to her sides, and Miles began to dissipate. As BUG consolidated, Meat barreled into the swarm. BUG tried to split but was hit with the full mass of Meat into the side of the dome splintering it. Cracks traveled up the wall behind Meat. Insects started to scurry out from behind him. There had to be an end game Loner thought. He looked towards the Balcony. He heard Gorge growl again. Gorge scrambled towards Loner. Franchise fired another two bolts into Gorge. No tendrils. He's out Loner realized. He peered over his shoulder. Meat slowly regained his composure and BUG was reconsolidating. He looked back at Gorge barreling towards him. He broke into a run. As Gorge wildly swung his arms and hands, Loner dropped into a baseball slide. As he slid under Gorge, Loner grasped Gorge's ankle. Loner quickly rose to his feet and jerked Gorge's leg, making him collapse on his face. Loner planted his back heel and leaned to the left again. He repeated the process he had just performed on Meat.

"I don't think that's gonna work twice," muttered Hopper to Fathom.

As he spun, Loner continued to peer over his shoulder. Now. He released the flabby monster. Gorge barreled through the air towards the spectators on the Balcony.

"Clever boy," Boss Winston said softly. In a panic, Dr. Monroe broke out in a run down the Balcony. As Gorge hit the Balcony, the protective barrier shattered, and shards flew inwards. The long, tan trench coat concealing Boss Winston fell to the ground. Gorge barreled through it and collided with the rear of the Balcony. A small white owl fluttered its wing out of the bottom of the coat and perched itself on top of the Engineer's armor.

"He's…a shape shifter…" Franchise said in awe.

"That's how he was never caught," realized Loner.

Gorge clambered to his feet snarling. The Engineer placed a solid metal boot on Gorge's backside and kicked him back down into the dome. Gorge tumbled and impacted with a thud. The owl flapped its wings and lifted off the Engineer. Midair, its shape changed and altered as Boss Winston placed his boots back on the floor of the balcony. He chuckled and slowly clapped his hands, acknowledging Loner's accomplishment. Gorge rose. Meat was back on his feet. And Bug had finished consolidating.

"Find a door," Loner told Franchise.

"But you can't lift it," Franchise answered.

"NOW!" Loner screamed.

Franchise fell into analysis mode. The room grew dark, and the edges of each door illuminated.

"THERE!" Franchise pointed.

"GET TO IT. NOW!" Loner yelled. The group scrambled to the metal barrier. The three monsters closed in on the heroes. "When I lift it," Loner started lowly, "run."

"But you can't," Hopper said without hope.

Loner reached into his back pocket of his jeans and retrieved two medical pens. He placed one in each hand, then forcefully pressed one into each leg. His eyes shot open. His hands quaked. He let out a primal yell as blood ran from his eyes and ears. He rhythmically curled in his fingers and arms. Shaking, he turned and dug his fingers into the metallic barrier. He screamed as spit flew from his mouth and the door rose slowly. With the door two feet off the ground, he screamed, "NOW!!! GOOOO!!!"

Afraid. Concerned. Mournful. Franchise pushed Fathom through. He grabbed Hopper and pushed him down, and he scrambled through. With one last glance, Franchise ducked through the opening and rejoined Fathom and Hopper. Loner released his fingers, and the metal barrier slammed shut.

"COME ON," Franchise beckoned.

"But Loner!" Fathom cried.

Hopper picked up Fathom, and he and Franchise start running down the hallway. Suddenly a figure appeared at the end. Franchise swung his crossbow upwards.

"Don't shoot!" a female voice called. Mirrors approached with her hands up in front of her face.

"Why shouldn't he?" screamed Hopper.

"I didn't know it was going to be like this! I swear!" Mirrors pleaded.

"Hit her Franchise," Hopper directed.

"I know where the girl is! I can show you!" Mirrors pleaded again.

"Lead the way," Franchise said in a low voice.

In the dome, Loner slowly turned. His body shook and trembled. "HA. GAH. HAH," he spat. The three monsters slowly approached.

"It was a good try son," Boss Winston congratulated Loner.

Loner reached into his other back pocket. In his trembling hands he held two additional medical pens. He looked forward through gritted teeth and a furrowed brow. He smashed the third pen into his

left shoulder. And the fourth into his right. The medical pens fell to the

ground. He leaned forward with his arms out to his sides and screamed, "GGRRREEEEAAAWWWW."

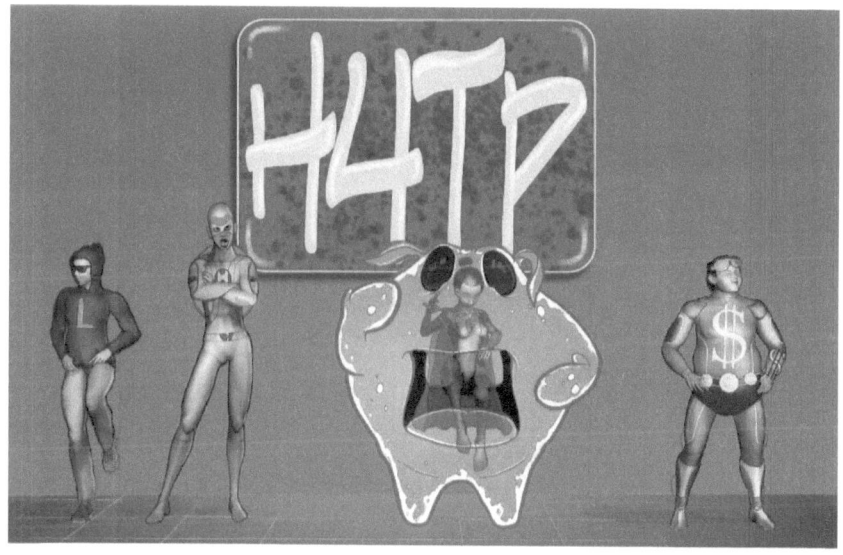

www.ingramcontent.com/pod-product-compliance
Lightning Source LLC
Chambersburg PA
CBHW020253200626
46816CB00001BA/266